PORCELAIN

RICHARD M PEARSON

First Edition

Typesetting by Leiah Ritchie
Cover Design by Ryan Tobias Thomas

BOOKBRAND.CO.UK

Porcelain is the sixth book by Richard M Pearson.

This journey started with the release of my first novel, *The Path* in 2018. It was initially planned to be a one-off, but life has a habit of taking you down a different road than the one you expect. There is a saying that everybody has one book to write and that was supposed to be mine. After some lovely feedback and positive reviews, I decided to do a follow-up called, *Deadwater*. From that point on I seemed to get a small but loyal cult following who encouraged me to keep writing. Each time I finish a new book, I feel it may be my last, who knows. All I can say is that writing has proven to be a journey with many twists and turns, just like my books I suppose. In fact, just like life.

I was born in England and then lived in Wales and Northern Ireland before finally landing in Bonnie Scotland at the impressionable age of eight. You could call me multi-cultural but in a homely sort of way. My stories tend to be based in Scotland, a country I have a deep passion for. Having said that, travel does make the heart grow fonder so I will occasionally take you to other dark and distant lands.

Reading has always been one of my great passions. I love books that build up a gothic atmosphere of foreboding, the first half of *Dracula* by Bram Stoker being a classic example. In my opinion, a good book should always have an unexpected finale. I will never forget reading *Rebecca* by Daphne Du Maurier and the way the twist turned the whole story on its head.

I hope that by the time you have finished this book you will have enjoyed the journey into the dark corners of your imagination. As I mentioned before, we all have the potential to write a book. Maybe mine will inspire you to give it a go as well.

Table of Contents

The Border country of Scotland will always be my spiritual home. I only lived there for a few short years, but I spent many more exploring its hidden beauty. Most visitors to the North speed along the motorway in a race to get to the glens and mountains of the Scottish Highlands. In doing so they miss out on a vast area of lonely forested hills, hidden towns, and quiet winding little roads.

It was a weeklong walk from Portpatrick to Sanquhar across the deserted hills and forests of Galloway that inspired me to write my first ghost story, *The Path*. I never did complete the second week of the trek that would have taken me through The Borders. I did not need to. Both this story and my last one, *Scotland Shall Burn*, are set in this gorgeous part of Scotland. The area exudes a feeling of the past as if time has still to catch up. The perfect setting then for this dark tale of drifting shadows and ghosts of the forgotten.

This book is dedicated to my mother and father, Maureen and Richie as well as my three sisters, Karen, Jacqui, and Mandy. As a family we have had our ups and downs but as you grow older one finds contentment and peace. My father passed away in 2011 and some of us have lost touch. The good memories remain though to drown out the trials and tribulations that all families must go through in life.

That day I set out on my bike for a week of cycling around the Borders I did not believe in ghosts. Maybe if I am being honest, I did not even believe in people anymore. For six days I charged headlong into relationships, friendships, and trouble. It was not just what was in front of me that made the journey so memorable. No matter who I met or where I ended up, she was always following in my shadow. At the time I had no idea who she was or what I had done to deserve the Porcelain lady hunting me down. I know now of course, but it is too late to save me. Guilt or reality? As the week went on, I lost the ability to know the difference. The one thing I always understood from the start was that the journey had to end with just the two of us confronting each other at long last.

LADY IN WAITING

Can I ask you to walk with me as the late evening sun dips behind the neat little suburban houses of Newton Mearns? There is still enough light, for now, to make us feel safe. I realise that dusk is creeping down on the earth but if we hurry then I can explain everything to you. I need to go back just this one last time. I can't do it alone; I will admit I am afraid. Please, just this one time, please I beg you, come with me.

The homes on Carrington Drive were mostly built in the early seventies. Many of them have been extended, some no longer even have that characteristic box shape that I remember when I was a child. The one thing that sticks out more than anything else are the trees and hedges. Over the years they have grown out of all proportion. Now many of the houses are drowning in a sea of untamed greenery.

I apologise if I have given you the impression that Carrington Drive is different from any other middle-class estate on the edge of Glasgow. It's not, the homes are no doubt occupied by couples with young children, or maybe older folks waiting for the time to come when they will have to downsize.

That is the thing about houses, they are really just conveyor belts. The young move in, they have a family, the children leave, and then they too are replaced by the next generation. As we make our way along Carrington Drive you can see the toys discarded on the lawn, bikes laying at an odd angle against the wall, and of course the obligatory child's trampoline covered in green mould. A Christmas present for the kids that was quickly forgotten about and left to ruin the lawn hidden beneath it. Yes, yes, everything looks normal as we pass along, well until we reach number 36.

It stands at the very centre of the bend in the road, the one that swings around and takes you back to where you started. When you think about it, this house could even be considered to be in the most desirable position in the street. It sits at the very top of our walk. It should be proud and dominant as it eyes its friends curving around towards it from either side. But that is the problem. Instead of being the King of Carrington, it hides behind two massive overgrown fir trees. Almost as though the building is ashamed to show itself to the rest of the houses.

Number 36 looks tired and worn. Not quite derelict but it certainly has an air of neglect. The whitewash on the pebble-dashed walls has a green haze creeping over it. The windows have not been cleaned for a few years. You can tell that the garden was once loved but now the overgrown rose bushes are matched in size and abundance by the weeds that sprout over every inch of space they can find. The large grey and green bins have toppled over and even though the brown one still stands; it is full of evil-smelling dirty rainwater.

Now, I know you are wondering why this particular house ended up so lonely and lost? The answer of course lies inside. I still have the key to the front door. Shall we go in and I will explain what happened? Maybe it is best that we hurry. I don't particularly want to still be around here once the sun finally dips below the horizon. The two large trees at the front tend to stand sentinel over number 36 these days. It is as if they want to bury the reason the house no longer wishes to be seen. The thing is it was her who planted them. All those years ago. The two tiny little plants have now grown into giants. Like me, they can't forget her. How could anyone?

The key turns in the lock and the handle moves down under pressure but the door does not budge. The changing temperature and constant Scottish rain have warped the frame. Can you help me push? There, it finally squeals open. We are in the kitchen already. These houses were built long before open planning and home design became fashionable. Strangely the back door goes out into the road while the posher front door with the hall faces onto a path. The seventies were strange times, you just need to watch the DJs on Top of the Pops to know that.

Inside it smells musty and damp. There is something almost human about a building. It is as though they need people, or they curl up and die. Even if the family living in the house do no maintenance, for some reason it still remains healthy but untidy.

But, once empty, the most loved home that has been well looked after will quickly disintegrate. Once the beating heart has walked out and locked the door for the last time all that remains is silence and ruin. Number 36 has only been unoccupied for two years and yet it feels like ten. We are walking through the kitchen now and into the living room. The furniture stands untouched. The walls and fireplace still have our pictures, her pictures hanging from them. The curtains are drawn, and the electricity has been shut off making it difficult to see the detail. I don't want to look. The memory hurts far too much.

Follow me out into the hall at the foot of the stairs. A pile of unopened letters and junk mail lies on the floor under the letterbox. Final demands, bills not paid, and endless pamphlets asking you to waste your money. The door has been boarded up just above the handle. Someone must have had to gain access without a key. I know you can feel my reluctance now. I don't want to climb the stairs to the upper level. It is getting darker, maybe we should leave? But we both know I have no choice. We have to go on. We have to find our bedroom, her bedroom. The one she hardly moved out of in the last few years. So much pain, so much hurt. I am at the foot of the stairs looking up. It seems so dark up there. I can feel her now, we are getting closer.

The top of the landing splits into four doors, all are closed. One is the bathroom, the other three lead into bedrooms. Two of these were only ever used for visitors. We never had children. Eve desperately wanted them, but despite our efforts, it never happened. Sometimes when I think back, I feel that was when her problem first started. It was soon after we were told that she would never conceive that the porcelain lady first appeared. From then on, she would come into our life with increasing regularity. The more Eve faded then the more I would catch glimpses of the ghost. She was subtle at first but then became bolder. I loved Eve, or at least what she had been. My God, I hated the Porcelain lady. I always will.

So, this is it. We have only one room left to go into. The bedroom where we once laughed, loved, cried, and held each other close. I can sense her presence. The walls may be damp and peeling but they still hold the smell and the touch of Eve. I can see her shadow floating around me. Long dark curls cascading over her face, the smooth white skin shimmering in the gloom. If only we could leave now and let me finish our exploration with a few grasped happy memories. I don't want to open this last door. I know what awaits. It was always that way during the last few years.

The room is almost dark. I spent so many years here living and caring that I can make out every shape from memory alone. The large mirror will be covered in dust, the dressing table will still have her things packed into each of the tiny drawers. It is the outline of the bed that I am staring at. I should be remembering the times when we were younger, the times when we had passion and we were in love. I can't though. All I see is Eve lying there waiting for me to move her, feed her, live her life for her. I try desperately not to look at the chair beside the bed. Not the one I would sit on and hold Eve's hand, the other one on the opposite side. Finally, I accept my fate. The way I always did. My eyes move towards the chair, praying, hoping that she has left. Of course, she is there. Why would she leave? The ghost has finally won. The day Eve departed the Porcelain lady moved in and never left. She is sitting on the chair. I know she is facing me. The shape of her eyes, her nose, and her mouth are in the exact places they should be on her face. But there are no holes. She cannot speak, she cannot hear, she cannot smell. The figure is moving now. It is starting to rise from the chair. Two years it waited for me to return. Will I never be free of her memory?

'I love you, Eve, I miss you so much.'

PAPER GHOSTS

SUNDAY

It was her eyes. When I wanted to communicate or feel close to Eve, they were the only thing she had left that remained part of what she once was. I bent down over the bed and kissed her forehead before picking up my rucksack and walking to the door. Kate was in the spare room. We had agreed the evening before that I would get up early, say my goodbyes to Eve, and then leave. Over dinner last night we had gone through the act. Me pretending I did not want to go and Kate reciprocating the charade by saying I deserved the break. The fact was, I was desperate to go, get out of my prison, be free for one last time. I had to make the pretence to Kate that it was a wrench to leave. She knew though. We both knew. Kate would have a week of lifting, wiping, feeding, watching, a week of being with somebody while also being alone. Before I stepped outside, I turned and shouted. 'That's me going now, Kate. Thanks again for doing this.' There was no answer from my sister-in-law. She was probably hiding behind the door desperate for me to go and save the two of us from any more awkwardness.

I wondered if she was watching me as I wheeled the bike down the front path. I doubt it, but I still walked slowly. Trying to make it seem as if I was going reluctantly. The reality was, as soon as I got to the end of Carrington Drive, I was gone. Like shit off a shovel, a whole week of freedom. Seven days of prison release for good behaviour. Surely, I deserved it? The last few years looking after Eve had become steadily harder. All our dreams, the multitude of plans, the chance to see the world in our retirement, so cruelly stolen from our grasp. What had been the point? You work like a bastard, take all that corporate bullshit and long hours to be able to retire at 54. The outcome, more money than you will ever need. Then Bang, all for nothing. You might as well burn the banknotes in the fire. They mean nothing.

As I edged the bike out onto the main road, I saw the crossing. Could it have been ten years ago, maybe more? I remember sitting in the car watching her walk out of the shop. It was the excited skip in her step that made me smile. The box with the shoes she had ordered were held tightly in her arms. Such a simple thing and yet it meant so much to her. I stopped the bike and stared, caught up in the memory. She was happy then, how I wish I could have captured that moment in a bottle. Kept it with me for the harrowing years that would follow.

I would love to pretend to you that I had meticulously

organised my weeklong cycling trip around Southern Scotland, but I would be lying. I messed about on the internet for a few hours and roughly worked out the route. From my Newton Mearns home on the outskirts of Glasgow, I hoped to bike the 60 miles to Moffat in the borders. Then over the next six days, my plan was to complete a circular journey of nearly 350 miles via Berwick and Carlisle to once again overnight in Moffat. I had agreed with Kate I would return late on Saturday or maybe Sunday if I got held up. We both knew it would be Sunday. Even if I had to sit at the bottom of the road for 24 hours.

I would have had a detailed plan if that useless bastard of a young brother of mine had come along as first agreed. Now he would not join me until Tuesday evening by catching the train to Berwick. I don't blame him for letting me down. I had talked him into coming along. I could tell he was only doing it because he felt obliged to. Guilt would drive him to take a week away from his perfect family and well-ordered life. I am going to bet you a tenner he does not turn up on Tuesday. Some excuse about a crisis at work or his wife Mandy needs to wash her hair. Sorry, I know I sound bitter, I don't mean to. I will still bet you that tenner though. No, let's make it a grand. One thousand pounds says he does not show up. Even in the unlikely event that I lose the wager, it won't matter. There is nothing left to spend my money on. I have nothing left, full stop.

It felt good to be peddling away, eating the first few miles up as I headed out towards Hamilton. I would be on busy main roads until I passed through the town. After that, it would be country lanes and finally the dedicated cycle track that followed the A74 south towards England. I was later getting away than I had hoped. Having checked everything the night before and then carefully packed my rucksack I discovered this morning that I could not find my phone. The bloody thing finally turned up in the bathroom. The very place I left it when I brushed my teeth. A quick glance at my watch showed it was 9 a.m. It didn't matter; the June sun would not set until 10 p.m. I suppose I should have booked a hotel in Moffat but that meant planning ahead. *To hell with all that, I needed adventure.* Anyway, I hate using the internet to spend money. It always feels like someone in Romania, or The Isle of Man will end up with my credit card details. It's not the cash, it's the thought of having to go through all that new card, new password shit.

The road was busier than I expected for a Sunday. Most of the cars rushing past gave me plenty of space. For some reason, a motorbike came up close beside me before racing away in a cloud of exhaust fumes. A few other cyclists passed by going the other way. I tried not to look at them as I hate that indecision you have to go through on whether to nod your head to acknowledge them or not.

The centre of Hamilton became my first stop. One hour done without mishap. I was so proud of the achievement that I decided to reward the effort with a coffee. I carried my purchase out into the pedestrianised main street and propped the bike against a shop window. It was a relief to take the heavy rucksack off my shoulders. The day was warm, but the first ominous dark clouds were drifting across the sky.

'Gan tae rain I reckon.' I nearly choked on my first gulp. There were plenty of people milling about but I hadn't noticed the old man who had edged up beside me. He was wearing a battered old suit and a white shirt with a blue tie. One of the last of the old school who would dress up to go to the shops. In his left hand, he carried a worn-out plastic shopping bag. His other hand was holding a roll-up cigarette which he placed between his lips after each statement. His craggy face would implode as he sucked the smoke into his lungs. His cheeks would become two craters for just that few seconds before the smoke would come billowing out. It was like watching a grotesque Rolling Stones concert. All dry ice and shrivelled skin.

'You park your car at the train station then son?' I looked at him and then my bike and the helmet I had placed on the saddle before replying with a hint of sarcasm.

'No, the car is tucked up in bed today, I am on a biking holiday. Heading down to the borders. First stop Moffat tonight.' He turned slowly to eye me up and down before taking another puff on his roll-up. His face was brown, a mix of sun-damaged lines and tobacco staining.

'Naw, ye wid be better getting a bus. Number 382 goes to Moffat from the station over by.' I took another sip of the coffee. It was in one of those paper cups with a lid and a tiny hole you drink through.

'Rains coming. Only a right dafty would bicycle with a storm coming.' I lifted my head and followed his eyes as he looked up to the sky. The coffee cup with the hole was attached to my lips and followed the same upward trajectory.

'Ye'll get soaked, the flood is comin.' At that exact moment, the lid came off the paper coffee cup and the warm contents poured all over my face. The brown liquid ran like a torrent down my new cycling outfit and onto the ground. It splattered over the concrete causing shoppers to jump out of the way. He was already shuffling off, puffs of smoke billowing behind him. The worn out old creased suit and the faded plastic bag. I know it was not his fault, but I still wanted to murder the old bastard. I was soaked. An hour into a weeklong journey and disaster had struck already. I knew I would dry out once I got going. It was the smiles and chuckles I could sense from the passing shoppers that were bothering me. And within an hour of leaving Hamilton, it started raining.

The first few miles as you head out of the large town involve a lot of twisting about on busy minor roads. I finally hit the B7078 and made my way towards Larkhall. The sky above was leaden and gloomy as the rain fell. To make things as uncomfortable as possible, the sun would occasionally pop out. I would be wet and warm but the minute I took my waterproof off the rain would reappear. In the end, I gave up and let the perspiration mix in with the water that dripped from my clothing.

Larkhall is one of those little Scottish towns that it's best not to cycle through with a green top on. Luckily, I was wearing a red one with blue stripes down the arms. Hopefully, the locals would think that the lack of green and the touch of blue meant that I sided with their town regarding the great Rangers/ Celtic divide. Anyway, I made it through unscathed, and after what felt like an eternity of torturous hills, I finally hit the open road again. The B7078 winds its way through small villages while keeping the M74 motorway within easy reach. The roar of busy traffic could be heard in the distance as it splashed through the rain-soaked tarmac.

It was a relief to reach the quaintly named village of Lesmahagow and finally arrive at the dedicated cycle path that would hopefully be my companion until I reached that day's destination, Moffat. The track is part of the old A74 trunk road to England that was superseded by the new motorway some years back. It meant I was now at last safe from cars and trucks as they raced past. Unfortunately, the rain was now coming down in torrents with no sign of letting up. The spray from my rear wheel was soaking through the rucksack on my back. I could feel the dampness permeating every inch of my body. *Why had I not checked the weather yesterday before I left?* In my defence, I suppose I just assumed that even if it was wet, well it was June. Surely it could not be that bad? *This is fucking Scotland you idiot, of course, the weather was going to kick you in the nuts.* There was only one thing left to do. For the next few hours, I put my head down and pedalled through the water.

The track twisted its way through an aptly named motorway service area called Douglas Water allowing me to take some respite from the rain. I chained the bike to a fence and trudged through the glass doors. Inside was a mass of humanity either queuing for the toilets or fast food outlets. They looked at me with disdain as a cloud of damp steam rose from my body and pools of water followed each footstep. It was hopelessly busy. My dream of a coffee and an old-fashioned log fire quickly vanished. The lines of travellers waiting to be served snaked around the tables and almost back out into the rain. *Come on, Grant. You can do this old boy. Let's get the hell out of here.*

I barged impatiently back through the human traffic in an attempt to escape. Unfortunately, my body burst through the glass exit door at the same time as a large leather-clad motorcyclist was trying to make his entrance. His burly hand caught me on the chest and sent me sprawling onto the wet floor. I jumped back to my feet ready to give the rude bastard some abuse, but his black motorbike helmet was already disappearing into the crowd. No-one stopped to help me, maybe a few looked with sympathy, but most had a queue to join. I no longer cared. I reached my bike and hurriedly tried to unchain it, desperation overpowering me. Maybe that was the problem. I had spent so long looking after Eve, just the two of us in eternity, now crowds crowded me out.

'North or South?' Two equally wet cyclists were standing

watching me battle to try and release the security chain on my bike.

'What?' I asked the question with a tone of incredulous impatience. *Who the hell would want to have a conversation about the direction in the middle of a monsoon?*

'Are you going North or South?' The man talking spoke in one of those old Etonian train spotter accents, if such a thing exists. I bet you his name was Roger or Stanley. The lady with him, who I assumed was his wife looked like Thora Hurd in cycling gear. I could tell they would be a well-matched couple.

'South, South, I am going South. Damn key won't turn.' Roger calmly stepped over and without invitation, he nudged my hand away and started twisting the key.

'Epra locks, they tend to stick in damp temperatures over 15 degrees. It's the humidity you see, and the gearing is also noted to be lacking in flexibility when wet. I read a very interesting article about it in this month's Bike magazine. Best take a three-quarter turn old chap then follow up with a full turn.' Of course, the lock gave way instantly, making me feel like a complete dick. Roger looked me squarely in the eyes and held the now free lock key out to me.

'Forget about going any further South today my good man. The roads flooded. We are going to try and make it to Lesmahagow and get a bed and breakfast. Weather is to improve tomorrow?' I jumped on my bike and pointed it towards the exit road making it obvious that I was in no mood to discuss travel direction in the pissing rain.

'Well, I'll just have to take my chances. Thanks for the help. Enjoy Lesmahagow.' I started to move away from Roger and Thora but not before he shouted one last bit of advice.

'Madness old boy, madness. Road is like a canal down there and getting worse. Better with a ruddy boat rather than a bike.'

***

I have this thing I do when faced with a hill on my bike. Often you cannot see the summit due to a bend in the road. I put my head down and then count each revolution of the peddles until they reach 100. I then take another look and do it all over again until I reach the top. Even the most serious hills are only about 500 revolutions at the most. That was until I met the climb of death just after leaving Douglas Water services. The first mile or so was downhill as the cycle track merged with the B road and dipped under the motorway. As I re-appeared out of the other side of the underpass, the track turned left. What faced me was a scene from the very depths of hell. Alright, I am prone to exaggeration, but it did look like a right bastard of a hill. There would be no point in doing my usual count of 100 and then looking up. This gradient was straight as far as the eye could see. By the time I reached the top, it would prove to be nearly 1200 revolutions. Not only was this bad enough, but rainwater was flowing down the tarmac in torrents. Maybe Roger was right, and I should have turned back but I would rather have drowned than give up my week of freedom.

To this day, I don't know how I made it to the top. A car coming the opposite way sent a wave of water over me that nearly knocked the bike from under my legs. By the time I reached the summit, I was utterly exhausted and wet through. For the first time that day, I realised that I was not going to make it to Moffat. I had to find somewhere to shelter for the night. This rain was not going to stop, and it was getting too dangerous to continue. I am sure a few miles further on Noah was already launching his Ark.

I knew the village of Abington was only 5 or 6 miles ahead and might have a bed and breakfast I could stay at. Even the thought of cycling that short distance in the driving rain felt like a hurdle too far. But the divine intervention was on my doorstep. My first bit of luck of the day had arrived, or so I thought. Up ahead in the middle of nowhere stood a long white building surrounded by an empty gravel car park. A sign on the B-road pointed to the worn-out structure. In faded letters, it said, *Douglas Inn*. I propped my bike up against the wall and trudged through growing puddles to the door. No lights shone; the place looked dead. Maybe Douglas was not in, after all.

I rattled the rain-streaked glass pane of the front door. All was dark and nobody answered. My decision was already made. If the place was empty, then I was breaking in. I placed my face against the door and tried to peer through. Condensation made it impossible to see anything. It was becoming obvious that the place was derelict. In my desperation to seek shelter from the deluge, I had hardly noticed the run-down state the building was in. The door would not budge despite my half-hearted attempts to force it. *Right, come on Grant. Let's check around the back of the building. There must be a window or something I can break?*

Even though it was a late summer afternoon, it was getting darker. Occasional rumbles of thunder could be heard in the distance as white streaks of lightning flashed through the clouds. This rain was not going to go away anytime soon and if it was possible, it seemed to be getting heavier. Drastic action was called for. I trudged around to the back of the building; it was in even worse condition than the front. It had several rear doors having once been a hotel but most of them had been boarded up. I swung my boot at the first one in frustration, nothing gave. It was at that point that I turned the handle and felt the door I had just attacked move slightly. I leaned against it and pushed, slowly it gave way. It was hard not to laugh. All this prowling around like a burglar and the door was not even locked.

I found myself in a long corridor with rooms leading off each side. At the end was a stairway to the upper level. The rain was battering off the roof but there was still enough light coming through the windows to allow me to explore. The place smelled damp and unloved. Old newspapers and litter were strewn across the floor. The lower part of the building comprised of a bar with the usual toilets and storerooms leading off it. A moulding pool table sat proudly in the centre of the main room watched over by dusty old framed photographs. Each one an image of long-forgotten faces holding trophies. A cobweb-covered dartboard hung on one wall with three darts all stuck in the treble twenty. Incredibly the bar still had some half-full optics of various spirits and a few bottles of unopened beer on the shelves. I made a mental note to check the dates on them later and headed off to explore the upstairs rooms. I hoped to find somewhere suitable to bed down for the night. At one time it looked like someone had lived on the upper floor. It was filthy, old wet clothes and discarded food containers lay everywhere. Empty vodka bottles sat scattered around a rotting old bed. Rainwater was dripping down the walls and damp stains covered the ceiling. Whoever had owned the place had lived in filthy squalor. I retreated downstairs to the relative safety of the bar.

***

It was seven o'clock in the evening and I was feeling pretty pleased with myself. The rain still came down in a deluge outside, but it no longer mattered. Further exploration had revealed a small room leading off the main bar. I now had a fire burning in the grate and most of my clothes and the rucksack were hanging over two old chairs to dry out. The rest of the furniture in the bar would be my firewood for the night. Everything was drenched. Even my phone had given up the ghost. The screen had a hazy condensation covering the glass. At least I would now be able to stick to my promise and not call Kate. Leave Eve to drift alone in that nether world of empty shadows and whispered dreams.

I crept back outside to bring my bike into safety. Even in those few minutes, it dawned on me what a lucky escape I had just had. The road next to the building looked more like a river. Nothing stirred, everyone and everything had taken shelter from the flood.

Leaving the bike propped up against the bar I explored the shelves. The beer bottles had expiry dates of February 2011. That meant the building had possibly not been used as a pub for around ten years. In one of the upstairs rooms, I had found a porn magazine from 2016. Whoever had owned this place had continued to live here for a while after the business had failed. A lonely man with his empty decaying building. His only company the naked girls staring out at him from the lifeless magazine pages, while downstairs the ghostly pictures of previous customers hung silently from the damp walls. I suppose I should have stopped for a minute and thought about the lost souls who had once laughed, cried, flirted, argued, and got drunk in the bar, but I was on a mission. An unopened bottle of whisky lay sideways on one of the shelves. Now I might not be Mastermind material but even I know that whisky gets better with age. *It was time to get the party started.*

***

Something was wrong. It felt cold and the little fire had gone out. I looked at my watch and could just make out the time, 3:15 in the morning. *What had woken me?* I could vaguely remember falling asleep around midnight huddled up in front of the flames. The orange glow casting dancing shadows on the peeling walls as I drifted into oblivion. A makeshift bed made out of my spare clothes and rucksack. I slept to the accompaniment of the rain bouncing against the roof. The ghostly echoes of a million drips as the water penetrated the old building. Luckily my little room remained relatively dry. The whiskey had done its business, my head hurt, and I still felt drunk. It suddenly dawned on me what had changed. It was the silence. The deluge was over, Noah had panicked and set sail in his ark, but I had survived.

I tried to get comfortable, but without the fire and whiskey to keep me company the little room had dropped its disguise. It was now back to its unhospitable best. Cold, dark, damp, and unfriendly. Suddenly my body froze. My ears strained to hear, all senses on alert. Something was creeping around behind the door. I lay perfectly still, terrified that whoever or whatever it was might slither over to my little room. Five minutes passed as I lay motionless like a frightened rabbit. *Maybe I had imagined it, get a grip Grant, you big baby.* The door handle creaked, just the slightest noise but now I knew for certain that someone was there.

'GET YOURSELF TO FUCK'

I screamed so loud that I damn near frightened the shit out of myself never mind whatever was in the building with me. Every nerve in my body was tingling with fear but adrenalin and terror forced me to jump up in the dark and throw myself against the door. Silence returned for a few seconds and then I heard it. That soft voice had haunted my brain so many times before. Always the same words, *I am still alive, I am still here.*

I was laughing hysterically at my cowardly stupidity. I had been through all this before. There was no one in the building with me. The voice was in my head, I knew that. Back home when I had first heard those words, I had convinced myself that it was Eve trying to communicate with me. Then one evening while sitting beside her bed I watched her, silent and incapable of speech or emotion, and yet the words still floated in the dead air.

I almost wished it had been the ghost of some long-dead customer. *Maybe we could have become friends, finished the whisky off, had a game of darts or pool?* I sat shaking for the next hour waiting for daylight and then fell into an uncomfortable sleep. I could see Eve staring at me. A smile on her face as she laughed at my stupidity before she was swept away back into the mist.

***

My phone showed it was 7 a.m. but the windowless room was still dark. I could still hear the occasional drip of dead water finding a passage into the building, but the rain was over. It felt warm as if summer had finally risen from the dead. Cleansed by the rain and black brooding skies of yesterday. I was in a good mood. Chuckling to myself at my cowardice over last night's imagined debacle. I desperately needed a drink of water to clear my head. Maybe I was still drunk, the fading buzz of the whiskey giving me an unusual optimism for what the day might bring.

I pushed the door open to let the light from the main bar flood in and grabbed my stuff together. My back hurt from sleeping on the rough floor and it did not help when I found my still damp spare clothes would not fit into the rucksack without strenuous effort. After much swearing and forcing it all eventually squeezed in. *Time to find water Grant old boy, there must be a tap somewhere in this dump.* I left the bag in the little room and went off on a mission to rehydrate my body.

Have you ever had that feeling when you see something, but your brain can't immediately compute it into reality? A few seconds of confusion, fear, misunderstanding, followed by the slow realisation and then stark horror. It was my bike. It was no longer leaning against the bar; it was perched on top of it. Well, when I say bike, I mean a part of the bike. The frame sat with the forks holding it in position. Both wheels had been removed, the retaining nuts placed neatly beside it.

I was still shaking as I sat on one of the old bar stools. At least logical thinking had returned rather than terror. Whoever had done this had simply taken revenge for me scaring the pants off them during the night. I had to accept there had been someone in the building with me after all. The voice was my imagination, but words don't lift bikes and take them apart. Maybe it had simply been someone like me, looking for safety from the rain. It was my own fault. But surely this was going too far. *Where the hell were my bike wheels?* I hoped to God that whoever it was had not taken them or broken them in an act of revenge. The thought of abandoning my adventure after one day would have been unimaginable. I could just see my brother Robbie sniggering with relief when I told him he would not need to meet me on Tuesday after all. The next hour was spent searching each room until I eventually found the front wheel in the upstairs bedroom. The weird bastard had placed it on the old bed. It was surrounded by individual pages of naked women from the discarded porn magazine I had found the day before. This guy was a nut job, all this just because I had not invited him to share the fire or drink my admittedly stolen whiskey. I looked everywhere for the other wheel to no avail.

Eventually, I took the search outside but again nothing. With the early sun casting its glow over the old building it was easier to take stock of the dilapidated state of the Douglas Inn. It was strange I had not noticed the large single red letter painted on the front door when I tried to break in the previous evening. A large E. I hoped not but somehow, I wondered if it was connected to my wheel thief? This was getting serious. The only thing left to do was phone the hotel in Moffat, the one I had booked for last night. Maybe they could send someone out to pick me up? There was little chance I would be able to buy a replacement without going to the nearest big town, either Dumfries or even Carlisle. It was a resigned and sorry figure that walked slowly back into the dank building.

I stood staring frozen in disbelief. The missing wheel was lying propped against my backpack. Fear overwhelmed my body as I realised the sick bastard must still be hiding in the building. He was playing with me, taunting me. I suppose you think I should have found a brick or a large lump of wood and gone searching for my tormentor. But no, instead I grabbed the bike, the wheels, and my stuff and ran like a scared rabbit out into the car park. I kept one eye on the job in hand and the other on the stark white building. Within half an hour I had re-attached the wheels and was ready to go. Nothing stirred, no sound came except the rustle of a light summer breeze. Whoever it was, he was good at hiding.

A tractor pulling a trailer could be heard trundling through the puddles out on the road. It pulled into the car park and an elderly farmer wearing waterproof overalls jumped down from the cab. 'The place is closed if you are looking for breakfast.' I decided it might be best to bluff things out as his tone and demeanour seemed less than friendly.

'Oh, that's a pity. I left Lesmahagow early this morning and was hoping to get a coffee here. Has it been closed down for a while?' He eyed me suspiciously as though he did not believe my story.

'Been closed ten years, but that's none of your business. You are on private property.' It was time for me to get the hell out of there before he discovered I had broken in.

'Ok. Sorry about that, I didn't realise. I will be on my way then.' He did not reply but started to walk towards the front door. I hurried off while stifling a chuckle to myself. *I hope the miserable old goat meets the phantom wheel stealer if he goes inside. That will teach him a lesson for being so rude.*

I walked the bike out onto the lonely road. Behind me stood the decaying sign pointing at the Douglas Inn. In front of me, the low sweeping border hills steamed gently in the new morning sun. The heat was starting to penetrate the long grass and tall fir trees causing a mist to blend into the hollows and contours. The earth was reborn and welcoming me to move forward. I did not look back at the building. It was dying, clinging to life just like her. Trying to hold me, *please don't go, I am scared. I don't want to die.* I was already flying, water spray from the diminishing puddles splashing around my legs. A free man, just me and the hills and the long empty road ahead. Glad to be on my way again. Happy to be safe from whoever had decided to torment me.

Eve

It seems so long ago now. I can recall the year but not the day, not even the month. Does it matter? As you grow older the footprint you leave behind becomes larger than the steps you must still walk. Memories blend into memories. A mass of faded images and forgotten emotion. Even the bad times become lost in the ether. No longer any more important than the happy times. Everything and everyone, including you are drifting into spirit. Finally making those last slow steps towards becoming the eternal ghost.

1989, yes that was the year. I was still in my twenties, three years down the road from the end of my last relationship. At first, it had been hard, that feeling of being discarded, dumped by the person you think you will be with forever. But time heals. Of course, it does. There I was standing on the balcony, a girl on either side of me. One of the few times in my life that I felt truly confident. One of them had a hand placed on the back of my jeans. Three figures staring out at the moon, drunk as lords. Inside the party was in full swing. A mass of twenty-somethings, either spoken for or searching for love. Hoping to make the connection before thirty arrived and the potential threat of eternal loneliness got its claws in.

Now don't get me wrong. I am no oil painting. The two

girls were old friends, we would flirt but nothing else. Single women were not exactly queuing to pick me from the display, but I was adequate enough to get noticed. We were talking and I was enjoying the attention when someone tapped me on the shoulder. I turned around expecting to see another drunken friend hoping to join the ménage a trois. A small figure looked at me, a silhouette surrounded by bright light and the thumping beat of eighties music. It took a few seconds for my eyes to adjust and take her in. It was the first time I had laid eyes on Eve. She stood there looking at me. Diminutive, long flowing black hair, a picture of perfection, both innocent and worldly. I knew even then as I stood motionless that I was already in love. She started to speak. The sound barely rising above the cacophony behind her. Maybe I could already read her lips, the bond was coming together so quickly.

'Would you like to dance?' Behind her was a Glaswegian party in full swing. People were bouncing around, 2 a.m. and it had reached the stage where everyone was dancing with themselves rather than a partner. She took my hand as the two girls watched and we danced while holding each other close. It was not even a romantic song. It could have been the Clash or the Cure, it did not matter. We had already started our own private party that would last for an eternity.

LIGHTBULB MOMENT

MONDAY

The sun was shining, I felt good. It always amazes me how quickly nature can restore itself to normality having just had a freak-out. The cycle track was still wet, but the puddles were already draining back into the earth. I would occasionally pass little rivers that had become loud and angry as they carried the flow back towards the sea. Very soon they would settle down again to become idyllic small streams, still and silent in the glowing sun.

My early start after the impromptu overnight in the Douglas Inn had helped me make up some lost time. I kept my head down and barely touched the brakes as the road climbed and then fell with monotonous regularity. Within 90 minutes I had covered 16 miles and arrived at the bottom of the next big climb. Even the sight of the famous Greenhillstairs could not dampen my spirits. The road into Moffat branched off to the left and crossed the M74 motorway on a shiny concrete bridge. All around me stood tall hills covered in statuesque fir trees. The main road and the railway followed the contours of the valley while up on the hillside stood countless tall windmills. The electricity generators of the future lined up like massive aliens staring down at their tiny masters below. The village I had intended to stay in was over the other side of the long gradient I now faced. It certainly looked like a 1000 plus revolution count. At least this time I would not be faced with driving rain and wind. Once I reached the top, I knew it would be a 4-mile freefall down into the village. An easy entrance just in time for breakfast. I yearned for coffee and something to eat. It was situations like this when I wished I had not made the jump into being a nonmeat eater. A bacon roll would have been perfect right now.

My planned rendezvous with Robbie in Berwick tomorrow would mean I would have to make up more than 60 miles today. At least it meant I would have a decent hotel to look forward to in Galashiels. No way was I intending on sleeping in some ruin again with a deranged intruder screwing around with my bike. Revolution after revolution passed as I kept my head down and slowly climbed the side of the valley. Even this early in the morning the sun was starting to heat the land. I could feel the sweat running down my back as I laboured towards the summit. At last, the road levelled out allowing me to stop and rest my aching limbs. The view was spectacular. Down below the motorway, B-Road and main line railway snaked side by side as they wound through the valley floor. Vast conifer forests covered the sides of the hills broken only by silver power lines carried aloft on tall steel monoliths. The cars and lorries on the motorway now looked like tiny insects. It dawned on me just how small the manmade footprint looked against the spectacular backdrop of nature.

My thoughts wandered back to happier times as I turned with anticipation to face the long descent into the village of Moffat. Ten years previously I had sat at this very spot with three friends. We had biked from Glasgow intending to stay over and then get the train home from the nearest railway station at Lockerbie the next day. The thrill of flying down the road had only been matched by the drunken antics of four middle-aged men let loose for one evening. How much easier life had been then. Just one short decade and everything had changed. The anticipation of returning home to Eve was now replaced with a sense of hopeless dread.

The bike was soon picking up speed without me having to peddle. With four miles of a sharp downward gradient to go, I was already touching the brakes after only a few hundred yards. It would be easy to run away on such a steep hill and I was in no rush to kill myself. Something felt wrong. I was gathering momentum too quickly and pressure on the brake handles was having little effect. In normal circumstances, I am sure I would have carried on desperately trying to slow the bike down. Within seconds it would have been too late, and disaster would have followed. But alarm bells were already ringing, something was telling me to act now or die. I pointed the bike into the grassy moss at the edge of the road and took my chance. Man, and machine bounced around in harmony for a few more seconds before the front wheel caught a rock and I was sent headfirst over the handlebars. A myriad of colours flashed around me as my torso somersaulted in mid-air before crashing back down to earth. I suppose it was one of those moments that people will say, *I saw my life pass before me.* Some life if you can see all that in less than a second.

I was sitting at the side of the road, a figure of utter dejection when I heard the sound of a motorbike coming up the Greenhillstairs. My shoulder hurt like hell but other than that I had been lucky. The soft moss had lessened the impact. I wish I could say the same about the bike. The front wheel was buckled, and I already knew the brakes were shot. Tears of frustration lined my face. *How unlucky can one guy be? First the monsoon, then the Douglas Inn stalker, and now my bloody brakes pack in.*

I needed help and I was angry. Maybe that was the wrong time for a motorbike to appear. Suddenly all my pent-up frustration exploded as the machine came into view. I was still holding a grudge against the rude bastard who had knocked me over at the service station. I ran out into the middle of the road waving my arms and shouting. It was one of those old-fashioned mopeds, driven by an older gentleman with an open-faced helmet. He pulled up and slowly switched the little engine off.

Only, it was not a man, it was a woman. As she removed the bike helmet her long white hair fell down around her shoulders. Catherine Houghton was slightly built and looked to be in her late sixties, and she was about to save my whole trip from disaster.

'You had an accident?' I looked at my mangled bike before replying.

'Yes, you could say that. Do you know if there is a bike repair shop in Moffat, or a car garage even? Someone who could help me?' She smiled and her whole face seemed to light up. They say you make up your mind about someone within seconds of meeting them. I liked her already and I was about to like her even more.

'My son, Barry repairs bikes in his spare time. He helps me to run the Bed and Breakfast, but I am sure he would come and pick you up.' I took a deep breath and tried to calm down even though I was still shaking.

'That would be brilliant, erm, sorry, what is your name?' She stepped from the bike and held her hand out.

'Cathy, Cathy Houghton. I own a B&B in Selkirk about 40 miles from here. I am sure Barry would bring you back to Moffat once the bike is fixed.' *Bring me back! Was Cathy crazy?* She had just solved my whole problem. I could overnight in Selkirk and that would leave me an easy 45 miles to get to Berwick and my rendezvous with Robbie tomorrow evening. Bingo.

'I don't suppose you have any vacancies for this evening, Cathy ?'

***

I watched as my newfound angel disappeared down the hill on her little motorbike. She had called her son, Barry to explain my predicament. I knew I was dealing with a professional when he asked what make of bike it was so he could sort out a replacement wheel. I just hoped the frame was not damaged as well. I suppose I could just buy another bike, but I was fond of this one. It might have tried to kill me, but we were still good friends.

It would take him more than an hour to reach me so rather than sit like a turkey at the side of the road, I started walking. It was four long miles to the village but at least it was downhill. I had barely gone a few hundred yards when I started to regret my decision. The only way to move the mangled bike was to hold the front end up off the road. The wheel looked more square than round and seemed to be the cause of much amusement to each passing car. I might as well have hung a big sign on my back that read, *Yes, I crashed my fucking bike*. One helpful young couple even tooted their car horn as they drove by. How nice, I thought, before giving them a V-sign as a thank you.

I must have covered a few miles before the little country road came to a T-junction. A sign pointed left to Edinburgh and right to Moffat. But it was not this that was attracting my attention. A rusty old blue Transit van was slowing up as it approached. It sounded as though the exhaust was broken as it clattered and banged to a halt. The massive bulk of Barry Houghton lumbered out of the driver's seat. My God, he was big. He was vastly overweight and immensely powerful looking. Lank straggly black hair ran down the side of his face and over his shoulders. He wore a gigantic pair of those trousers you see fishermen in, held up by braces. He ignored the other traffic trying to weave past his now stationary old van and walked up to me. I swear to God, he was so large, his frame was causing an eclipse of the sun.

'Barry, my name is Barry.' He held out a big rough hand and smiled. He had that same infectious friendly grin that his mother had. I know this sounds terrible, but I could not help thinking, *how the hell did that tiny woman produce this man-mountain?* He picked the bike up and cast a professional eye over it.

'Looks to be ok except for the wheel. What happened, you try to come down the hill too fast?'

'No, for some reason my brakes failed. I don't know why as I had it fully serviced before I left Glasgow.' Even though I was probably twice his age I felt like a stupid schoolboy making excuses in front of a teacher. He ran his giant hand down the front wheel as though he was a doctor probing for the answer before he looked at me and grinned once more.

'Grease. That's your problem. Why did you put grease all over the wheel? No wonder your breaks don't work buddy.'

I walked over to the passenger door of the rusty van and pulled it open. My mind was racing. *That bastard last night.*

Not only did he remove the wheels, but he then greased the bloody things up. Why? What the hell did I ever do to deserve that?

Within minutes we were clattering along the remote A708 linking Moffat to Selkirk. Bike parts, discarded food wrappers, and cigarette ends littered the cabin floor. It was a good job that the van had three front seats because the big guy took up almost two of them. He drove like a maniac with one hand on the steering wheel while the other simultaneously juggled chocolate bars and a lit cigarette. Big Brian obviously knew the road because he rarely looked at it while he regaled me with stories of biking accidents and life in the Borders. I suppose I should have been scared but his enthusiasm was infectious. I settled down contentedly amongst the refuse and let life wash over me. I never did get that breakfast in the village but by good fortune, my trip was back on track. Catherine Houghton and her herculean son had come to my rescue. Little did I know that this was going to be a case of, out of the frying pan, and into the fire.

***

It was hard not to smile as I lay on the bed. Ok, I must be the most crap cyclist in the world, but at least I was a contented crap cyclist. In two days, I had biked a total of 54 miles rather than the 100 that had been planned. Instead of overnight stops in Moffat and Galashiels, it had been a cold bed in the derelict Douglas Inn followed by the prospect of a comfortable sleep in Ettrick Guest House just outside Selkirk. Tomorrow it would be an easy 40 odd miles to Berwick. I could leave at ten, have a hearty breakfast, and meet up with that dopey young brother of mine in the evening. Of course, I would not mention the free ride. I would tell him how hard the 140-mile slog had been. Lay it on thick how I had braved a monsoon and a night in a deserted building just to make sure I made our planned rendezvous. I had no intention of mentioning the friendly intruder or the accident. He would have just given me that look, the one that meant he was superior, and that I was a useless waste of space.

My eyes scanned the room. It felt musty and damp. Odd ornaments filled every potential space. Cats made of porcelain, silver-plated jugs, cheap mats, coasters with vague Chinese designs, and wall pictures of all different shapes and sizes. Nothing matched. Why was I not surprised? The minute I had stepped into Big Brian's van I somehow knew that he and his tiny mother would not be operating The Ritz in Selkirk. It was a large building; at one time it must have been an impressive house but now it looked run down. The smell of stale fried breakfast permeated the building. The rooms did not even have their own bathroom. You had to share with the other occupants on the same floor as yours. I had taken a shower while at any minute expecting to hear a rattle on the door by someone needing to take a pee.

'Hi, I am Mrs. Leadbetter from Dorking. I am desperate, would you mind? It's ok, you can continue with your shower, just ignore me. My husband Donald will be along shortly.

Brian collected cars or should that be scrap cars. The garage at the side of the building was littered with rusting old hulks and engine parts. And yet I had noticed a few newer motors parked at the front and had been surprised to hear that Ettrick House had other customers. Maybe they were from London, that would explain it.

It was still only mid-afternoon, and I was bored. The building was perched in isolation at the side of the minor road from Moffat just before it joined the busier A708 into the small town of Selkirk. What I am trying to tell you is, there was fuck all to do. Enquiries to Mrs. Houghton had revealed the Ettrick Guest House did not have a bar. 'We can give you a bottle of beer but most of our guests don't drink so we don't have an actual bar as such.'

'Oh, I just fancied an hour or so in a local pub. Is there one near?' I was lying about the hour. I fully intended to get drunk and stay as long as possible.

'Brian could run you into Selkirk if you want to go for something to eat or a drink. The other option is to walk back up the hill to the pub in the village of Arrowford. It's only a mile away.' What a thoroughly helpful old lady she was. I loved the way everything she did seemed to involve her giant son doing the work.

My thoughts drifted back to Eve. I still loved her, well I still loved what she had been. It felt wrong to be feeling so happy, so free of burden. In five days, I would be back. The torment would start all over again. I could hear the keys to the jail turning already. Not only that, my shoulder still ached from the fall off the bike. I needed alcohol.

To hell with this. No point in wasting the day Grant old boy. I was already lifting myself off the bed as I spoke the words. *Let's see if mountain boy is up for taking me to Selkirk, maybe I could even buy him a pint.*

I grabbed my bike jacket and headed down the stairs and out into the bright sunshine. A drilling noise was coming from the garage at the side of the house. I weaved my way through rusting cars and bikes and knocked on the door. The sound of a man at work continued so I assumed he could not hear me and turned the handle to step inside. The place was dimly lit by single unshaded light bulbs hanging down from the ceiling every few yards. Everywhere was covered by old metal shelves stacked high with a myriad of assorted mechanical parts. Bike wheels and inner tubes hung from nails on the walls, the smell of paraffin and dead engine oil hung in the stale air. I crept gingerly through the gloom until I could just make out the massive bulk of Big Brian standing with his back to me. He was bending over a lump of metal that was held in a vice. Suddenly sparks showered around him from the blow torch he held in his mountainous hands. His frame had become silhouetted in a bright glow that made him stand out in the dank surroundings.

He was wearing a dress, one that was so obviously short for him that it rode grotesquely up his back to reveal stockings and what looked like suspenders. The scene was not helped by the fact that woman's knickers didn't come in his size. A massive pair of wellington boots covered his feet and the long greasy black hair down his back was tied into two ridiculous-looking ponytails. He was whistling away to himself while he worked. I edged out backwards without making a sound. I felt happy for Brian, he seemed so contented beavering away in his workshop kingdom. But call me old-fashioned if you want. I suddenly felt that a walk into the village of Arrowford seemed like an easier option than asking the big man for a lift.

***

The little road climbed steeply as it burrowed its way through the hill that backed onto Ettrick House. I don't know why but just before I lost sight of the building, I turned around to give it one last glance. Someone was looking out of one of the first-floor windows. It was difficult to tell but the figure seemed to be a woman. I had this odd feeling that it was my room although I was not sure which window was mine. I shrugged and turned to walk on. Maybe it was old Cathie Houghton turning back the bed sheets ready for me when I staggered back later on. What a nice woman she was.

Despite the summer sun floating brightly above, the hedges and trees cast a shadow as they clung tightly to the narrow lane. The heat and claustrophobia soon started to work their dark spell into my good mood. It was not the big boy's poor dress sense that was annoying me, it was Mrs. Houghton saying it was only a mile to the village pub. *A mile! I was sure I had walked three already and still no sign of that longed-for beer. Ok, maybe I exaggerate, and the heat was getting to me, but it was more than a mile, I kid you not.*

At last, a few buildings came into sight as I rounded yet another bend in the road. Very soon I was walking through the small but picturesque settlement of Arrowford. A neat row of cottages sat on either side of me, colourful flower gardens baked in the sun. My spirits were soaring again, I could almost taste that cool pint of lager. And then within minutes, I was at the end of the village and no sign of any pub. In fact, no sign of anything except neat little houses and flowers. My spirits suddenly dropped from the sky and into one of the drains at the side of the road. That first impression I had of liking old Catherine Houghton was being severely tested. First of all, a mile had turned into ten and now the bloody pub did not exist.

An attractive middle-aged lady with long thick black hair and a matching dog on a lead was approaching as I turned to walk back. This was my last chance of salvation. I felt self-conscious as I went to speak.

'Hi, lovely day for a walk. I don't suppose there is a pub or a café in the village? I am dying for a cup of tea.' She looked me straight in the face and smiled.

'Oh yes, The Arrowford Snug, take the lane on the left near the bus shelter.' I wanted to kiss her but thought better of it.

'Oh great. Heavens above it is warm today. Thanks for that.' I bent down and patted the dog. Both of us knew that it was obligatory for a stranger to fawn over another stranger's dog. It was cute though even if it did slaver all over my hand. I started to walk nonchalantly back towards the bus shelter as though the pub was not important to me. I could feel her and the dog watching and smiling.

'I don't think they serve tea; you might have to have something stronger instead.' I pretended I had not heard her and kept on going.

The Arrowford Snug was hidden away down a lane, no signs pointed to it. It didn't even look like a boozer. It could have just been another village cottage basking in a kaleidoscope of colourful flowers and the sweet aroma of summer. The only admission it made to being part of the licensing trade were the letters on the door that spelt out BAR. I had the feeling that this place was for the villagers, not hopeless Glaswegian cyclists on the run from everything and everyone. I pushed the door open with little expectation other than hopefully having a nice cold beer. Maybe that is the positive thing about being a pessimist. If your glass is only ever half empty, well then if someone in life suddenly refills it you get a pleasant surprise. Surely that is better than being eternally disappointed? The Arrowford Snug was indeed perfection in a nice tall glass.

***

'Same again chaps?' I lifted the three empty pint glasses and strode to the bar. My words had been a statement rather than a question. Jocky and Lugar Tam had already bought two rounds each. Their insistence on buying me drinks had only been matched by their good-natured banter and friendly welcome. The bar was not large but it exuded atmosphere. I was surprised to find it so busy on a late Monday afternoon. Around twenty customers squeezed into the small room. Three oak tables with chairs and half a dozen bar stools made up the furniture. A large unlit fireplace backed onto the rear wall. The beer buzz was thriving as the mostly male audience chatted about everything and nothing. Two young couples sat together in deep conversation at one of the tables.

'Three pints of lager please.' The barman was for some reason called Wendy. A tall well-built middle-aged man with a thick beard. He reminded me of a sea captain. I had assumed it was a pub joke but even though I was now merry I could not bring myself to say his nickname.

'So, you are from Glasgow then? Are you staying in Selkirk tonight?'

'Yes, yes, I am booked into Ettrick Guest House.' He turned and said something in reply as he poured the beer. The chatter from the rest of the customers made it difficult to make out his words.

'Sorry, erm Wen, erm sorry I didn't hear you there.' He leaned forward and placed his face just inches from mine while the cool lager flowed into the glass from the tap.

'That's a coincidence, small world.' He shouted the words so I could hear them.

'Oh, you know Mrs. Houghton then, nice lady.' He stepped back to take the full pint and placed it on the counter before grabbing another empty glass to start the process over again. Once more he spoke, and I could not hear. This time I didn't need to reply as he quickly realised the situation and once again leaned forward.

'Her son, her son Barry. He's my wife. We got married in Edinburgh last year.'

I sat listening to Jocky and Lugar Tam for another hour or so until a fourth friend arrived. Big Notty was as friendly as the other two and very soon he had joined the round and was supplying me with more beer. Occasionally Jocky would check to see if Wendy was looking before sneaking a half bottle of whisky out of his coat pocket. He would proceed to pour a little bit of the liquid into each of our beer glasses. Of course, I was getting drunk and, in the morning, I would regret it, but I was happy being out again. Once more enjoying easy-going male company after way too long.

'I always fancied getting a bike, heading up to the hills.' Lugar Tam's words were met with chuckles from the others. Big Notty waded in next.

'Aye, I could just see you on a fecking bike Tam. Ye cannie even get on a bus ya useless big eejit.' A chorus of laughter followed, even from the victim of the joke, Lugar Tam. But I was only half listening. My eyes had turned to the door as it opened, and a tall figure strolled in. He was decked out in black motorbike leathers and still had a matching dark helmet covering his face. He looked more like an alien as his heavy boots clunked towards one of the bar stools and he sat down with his back towards me. Maybe the beer was clouding my judgement, but I could not help thinking he looked very much like that big bastard who had pushed me over at the service station the day before.

The good-natured chatter and jokes at each other expense continued while the clock ticked on into the early evening. The sound of voices and glasses clinking was becoming louder and more animated as the alcohol flowed. New arrivals through the door would be loudly welcomed, it seemed everyone knew everyone else. I sat there getting ever more inebriated, but I no longer felt part of the group. I half-listened to the conversation about football, politics, Lugar Tams wife who wore the trousers in his house, life in the village, Wendy and Barry, but my attention was on him, Leather boy. He sat with his back to me nursing a diet coke in his hand. The motorbike helmet on the bar beside him. Occasionally he would say something to Wendy while every few minutes turning and pretending to look at the door. I knew It was really me he was giving discrete sideways glances too. I was convinced it was him. He perfectly matched the picture I had in my head of the guy who had pushed me. Tall, head to toe in leathers and motorbike boots. His hair was grey, cropped short. I found it hard to read his age, maybe mid-forties. It was definitely the same guy. I just knew it. *Maybe it was even him who had crept around the Douglas Inn last night. Yes, that's it, he must have followed me from the service station. That's him, the bastard who took my bike apart.*

'Grant, Grant. For feck sake man, will you pay attention? You are the neutral here. Who is the boss in the Lugar Tam household, him or his misses?' The question was followed by laughter, but I was already starting to rise from the table. The alcohol clouded my brain as I stood up too quickly and staggered forward. The others assumed I was going for a pee and laughed even harder as I lurched in the direction of the bar. I was drunker than I realised as my body weaved haphazardly towards its intended target.

It is hard to recall exactly what happened next. I believe I tried to swing a punch at Leather boy just as Jocky attempted to grab me. Unfortunately, or maybe, fortunately, I missed, and the momentum of my arm sent me and Jocky tumbling to the ground. One of the tables occupied by two lovely young couples went crashing along with us. Bacardi Breezers and fresh orange juice splattered over them and the two falling figures. The odd thing I recall is the few seconds of silence that followed. Suddenly the Arrowford Snug had gone completely quiet. It was probably my only proud moment of the whole scenario. Leather boy was quickly on his feet, his faced purple with rage. He looked enormous standing over me. Within seconds he had lifted me bodily off the floor and placed his big red face within inches of mine. My feet hardly touched the ground as fresh orange dripped down my chin.

'You fucking idiot bastard. What the hell are you playing at.' I suppose I should have been ashamed, but it was only when I turned to look at the lady standing beside him that real remorse hit me. It was the black-haired woman with the dog who had pointed me in the direction of the pub only hours earlier. She was pulling Leather Boy's hands off my throat, but it was the words that stung.

'Leave him, Lawrence. Can't you see, he is just an old drunk. It's not worth it. Put him back down in the gutter where he belongs.'

Seconds later Wendy had virtually thrown me out through the entrance door. Grant Ramsey has left the building. I suppose I had to admit that my Douglas Inn intruder and Leather boy were probably not the same people. Why the hell does alcohol make some ridiculous notion seem perfectly reasonable?

It was still daylight, but the evening was moving on. Dusk was creeping up slowly as the sun descended towards the horizon. I wondered if it had decided to hide after hearing about my behaviour in the Arrowford Snug. Even the big yellow ball in the sky was embarrassed for me. And yet, I was no longer ashamed. I was still drunk as I weaved my way down the hill back to the Ettrick Guest House. Jocky had insisted on walking me back, I think he felt responsible for getting me so drunk. We were laughing our heads off while Jocky passed the remains of the half bottle of whiskey between us.

'That is the funniest thing I have ever saw Grant old boy. What the feck made you try to lamp big Ollie?' I had already decided not to mention my previous encounter with a motorcyclist, so I just shrugged and returned the laughter.

'I do feel bad Jock. Poor guy and his wife just out for a quiet drink and I try to bloody lamp him.' Jocky stopped in the road and pulled my arm towards him. His red ruddy cheeks glowing with the beer and whiskey.

'Are you fecking serious Grant? You will be forever famous in Arrowford. That big tool Lawrence Kirkland and his snooty wife Barbara deserved it. He ponces about telling everyone how fucking rich he is. Bloody big eejit should grow up, acting like a teenager in his leather pants.' I laughed, Jocky was making me feel better about myself already. Suddenly I was no longer an old drunk who deserved to be in the gutter, I was the hero of Arrowford.

'Anyway, after what you have been through with your poor wife Eve, you deserve a blow-out. Don't give yourself such a hard time man.' The words he had just spoken sank deep into my heart. I was crying, tears streaming down my face. Tears of inebriation, tears of frustration, tears of desolation. What the hell was I doing out here? I should have been with Eve, the two of us doing what older couples do. Supporting each other, walking hand in hand, staying in a nice hotel. Suddenly I felt like I was back to being an old drunk, back in the gutter once more. Jocky put his arms around my shoulders and hugged me. He understood. Only two equally drunk men can see the world in the same light as each other. He finally left me as we walked around the last corner and the lights of Ettrick House shone out in the descending summer gloom. I watched him as he disappeared back to the village and the evening's scandal. I would never see him again or Lugar and Big Notty, but I knew I had made my first new friends in years.

I pulled my phone out of my pocket. It was working again after being soaked in yesterday's downpour. I needed to call Kate, find out how things were with Eve. I was shocked to see it was nearly ten o'clock. What the hell had happened to the last six hours? It was too late to call and anyway, why break my promise not to make contact? What was the point? She would just tell me, *Eve is laying here, motionless, doing nothing. The way it always is now.* The phone was already back in my pocket as I crunched up the gravel driveway towards the big house. There was now only one visitor's car near the front door, but something else held my attention. A big shiny black motorbike was sitting opposite it. A massive silver chain draped through the front wheel. In the dark, it reminded me of the devil himself, but hey, I was drunk. I already told you how inebriation makes the ridiculous seem normal.

Eve

I had my first date with Eve the following weekend after the party. As she left to go home, I asked for her phone number. She made some excuse why it would be better for her to phone me instead. You have to remember that this was 1989, mobile phones for the masses had yet to be invented. You could still go to a telephone box and insert coins into little slots. There was even a nice lady you could speak to known as the operator. She would fall for the free phone call scam every time.

'Hello, is that the operator?'

'Yes, how can I help you?'

'I just put ten pence into the slot and the telephone ate it up without connecting me.'

'Ok Sir, what was the number you were trying to call, and I will connect you.'

It was not all fun using a telephone box though. They invariably smelled of urine and more often than not the telephone would be missing or broken. Anyway, I digress, I had a landline in my flat and for the next week, I sat waiting for the call. By Thursday it had still not arrived, so I phoned around a few friends who had also been at the party. I finally found someone who knew who Eve was, in fact, they worked in the same place as her. I was told that she liked me and would call. I kid you not, I put the receiver down and the phone rang out within seconds.

'Hello, is that Grant. We met at the party last weekend.'

We arranged to meet that Saturday evening in a pub in the Southside of Glasgow. I was already standing at the bar ordering my second beer hoping to overcome my nerves when she tapped me on the shoulder. The place was busy and noisy, but she seemed to float in from another world. Beautiful, transient, friendly but at the same time detached. We slowly got drunk together while trying to shout over the din. The evening wore on and soon became a haze of cigarette smoke, voices, and background music. We remained lost in our own small world until suddenly it was 11 p.m. I plucked up the courage to ask her back to my place and was overjoyed when she quickly responded with a yes. But it was from this point that things went pear-shaped.

Of course, I did not know her background at the time. If I had then I would never have suggested using the shortcut that ran alongside the river. I was relatively well known in those days and for some reason, I decided it would be best not to cross paths with any of my acquaintances on the way home. It was pub chucking out time in Glasgow and I was worried who we might bump into. It was too soon for her to meet Squarejaw Bob or heaven forbid, Manky Joe the dealer.

'Hey Grant, how ya doin man. Who's the wee burd, nice? You wanting anything tonight? I just got a new supply in, fucking solid stuff man.'

I am sure Eve would have laughed it off, but I was trying to make a good impression. We walked down the steps and onto the river path. It was dark, only the occasional ancient streetlamp shone through the gloom. Maybe it was the alcohol in my blood, but I thought I could hear someone following us. Eve was becoming more nervous with each step. She let go of my arm and started to walk ahead as though she was in fear of her life. Now I too was nervous because of her reaction and the ten-minute walk along the dark lonely riverside path seemed to take an eternity. We finally reached the stairs that would take us back up to street level. Eve spied a taxi rank and ran over to it.

'What's wrong, Eve? My flat is just around the corner.' She was looking at me as though I was a murderer. And yet, something still sparkled in her eyes. Some recognition that maybe she was overreacting, and maybe I really was a nice guy.

'I will call you.' She jumped into a taxi and was gone. I walked back to my flat alone. How was it possible to go from such a high to the depths of despair. She didn't phone and for two weeks I spent each day at work feeling miserable and lost. There was only one solution left for me. I knew she lived in a flat with her sister on the North side of Glasgow. I even remembered the name of the street but not the number. Exactly 14 days later I was boarding a train into the centre of the city ready to find my fallen angel.

THE DEAD HOURS

TUESDAY MORNING

I was standing in front of a waterfall, clear blue and ice cold. It crashed down onto the rocks sending shards of misty spray into the air. I could almost touch it, but it remained just inches from my outstretched hand. If I took a step forward it would take a step back. Pure liquid gold tempting me to follow but always just out of reach.

I woke in the pitch-black room; my tongue was stuck to the top of my mouth. I desperately needed a drink of water, anything to quench this alcohol thirst. I still felt drunk as my arm reached into the darkness to see if my phone was on the bedside cabinet. *Please tell me I did not lose my mobile last night.* My fingers found the little switch on the lampshade and a dim light flooded into the room. I was still fully clothed; I had not even managed to take my shoes off or get under the duvet. *Oh boy did I need a drink of water.* There was not even a sink or a kettle in this excuse for a guest house. The phone was nowhere to be seen but a dusty clock ticking away on a chest of drawers stated it was a quarter past two in the morning. My only hope was to stagger to the shared bathroom for salvation. Vague memories of last night's escapade floated back into my head. *Why did I no longer feel like the hero of Arrowford? Why the hell did I drink so much last night?*

The journey to the bathroom was conquered without mishap. Well not without a few stumbles along the way, including knocking over a small table on the landing outside my door. I just hoped the other two rooms I shared this floor with didn't have any customers in them. A dim modern-looking nightlight was the only aid to finding the toilet. Before leaving the bedroom, I had searched high and low for my mobile. I remembered having it when I arrived back at the Guest House only hours before. *Maybe I had dropped it outside. Hopefully, it would be found in the morning.*

The bathroom felt cold and uninviting. Faded green tiles with a flowery pattern lined each of the walls. The grout was black from the damp caused by the shower being in constant use. Unfriendly-looking yellow and blue towels hung limply over the edge of the bath. I stuck my head under the cold tap and opened my mouth to drink in the ice-cold liquid saviour. It was warm, very warm, causing me to jerk back in disgust. *Jesus, even the bloody taps in this dump are the wrong way around.* I turned the one with a red mark on it and it also shot a deluge of warm water into the sink. I felt too dehydrated to care; within seconds I was gulping the foul-tasting liquid deep down into my body.

The stagger back to my room went without any further disasters as I kept my tired red eyes focused on the worn brown hallway carpet. Something was different. I could sense a change in my surroundings in the few minutes I had been in the bathroom. A large pair of motorcycle boots sat outside the door next to mine. I was sure they had not been there before. *What was it with this trip and motorbikes?* I was beginning to feel as though I was being haunted by the ghosts of lost Hell's Angels. My body was too tired and hungover to care. Anyway, I had made enough of a fool of myself with the biker in the pub. The best bet was to let this one sleep and ignore the poor soul.

My hand reached for the handle of the bedroom door. Somebody was standing at the other end of the corridor barely noticeable in the gloom of the night light. It looked like a young woman with her back to me at the top of the stairs. I decided the best thing to do was get back inside my room. *Who the hell walks about at this time of night?* I suppose I had a nerve asking the question as I was doing exactly the same thing. *Maybe the poor lady had a hangover the same as me and was searching for the bathroom?*

The missing phone was sitting in the middle of the pillow. How it got there I have no idea. There had to be a logical explanation. *Maybe I was losing my mind, maybe I was still drunk.* I pulled my clothes off and crawled under the covers. Sleep would be the only thing to stop this weirdness. The bright morning sun would erase the mess of the previous day and let me start again. Slowly the world around me merged into cascading flashes of colour. My brain started drifting into that nether world of confusion and dreams. Eve, motorbikes, the myriad of odd ornaments dotted around Ettrick House, taps that only dispensed hot water, yellow and blue towels, strange women walking about in the middle of the night, sleep, sleep, sleep.

I woke and the room was still pitch-black. My tongue was still stuck to the roof of my mouth, and I still desperately needed a drink of water. My arm once more reached out to switch on the little lamp but this time my fingers found the phone. I fumbled for the on button and stared incredulously at the display. 2:15! That was impossible. I had already been up at that time to go to the bathroom. I distinctly remembered the haphazard trip to the land of damp-smelling yellow and blue towels. I shone the handset light across the room towards the dusty clock on the chest of drawers, it too showed 2:15. *Jesus, it's the clock. The bloody thing is like everything else in this place, broken.* The logic in my head told me that the clock was stuck at the same time. I had obviously gone to the bathroom earlier and now it really was 2:15. How slow was this night going? I could still hear it ticking away, and yet, why did it sound strange? Tap, tap, tap, rather than the soft mechanical beat of time. I shone the light above the clock and it slowly hit me that the noise wasn't coming from the clock at all, it was seeping through from the wall to the room next door. The one with the motorbike boots outside. I eased my body slowly out of the bed making sure to make no noise, my eyes trained on the space above the clock. Tap, tap, tap. Rhythmic, like the march of time.

It took six intricate slow steps to reach the wall, I counted each one. Desperate to make sure I would not be heard I crept the last few inches and placed my ear against the wall. Tap, tap, tap. Whatever it was, it was coming from the next room. The dusty clock on the chest of drawers was still ticking away, the two sounds perfectly countering each other. *Maybe there was a water leak somewhere?* There had to be a logical explanation, and yet, no matter how I tried to convince myself, I still could not get away from the feeling of dread. It sounded human. As though someone in the room next door was tapping the wall deliberately. *It was after two in the morning, why would anyone want to torment me?* And then I did the most stupid thing imaginable. Maybe this whole trip and leaving Eve was playing with my head. I was acting irrational, I knew it, but then had this whole trip not been messed up from the start? I placed my mouth close to the wall and spoke.

'Who are you?' The tapping suddenly stopped. I was staring at the wall like some sort of stage-struck idiot. The clock ticked for a few more seconds, I felt like laughing at my stupidity. And then the familiar words floated through the wall. Only this time the woman's voice was no longer the soft whisper I had come to expect. Now it was harder, deeper as if it was mired in sadness and torment. *I am still alive; I am still here.* The words cutting through the masonry and paint, arriving in my head in a cloud of dust and dead insects. It felt like something was gripping my throat, choking my life away while the clock ticked up my last seconds on earth.

I staggered back in horror from the wall. Watching the chest of drawers and the clock as though they might at any minute spring to life and attack me. A grown man acting like a frightened child as I crawled into the bed and pulled the duvet over my head. *For heaven's sake Grant. Get a grip of yourself man. This is a ridiculous way to act.* I promised myself that I would never drink again if this was the state it was getting me into. The last thing I saw before drifting into a fitful sleep was the clock face. It now showed 2:20. Tick, tick, tick, but at least the tapping sound was no longer joining in the chorus.

***

I was propped up against the pillows and staring at my phone. Scrolling through the apps, trying to eat up the hours until breakfast. It was 4:30 in the morning. Outside the first dim hint of the early dawn was challenging the dark night. I had woken an hour earlier and no matter how hard I tried; it was impossible to get back to sleep. At least the hangover was not so bad although I was desperate for a drink of water. I knew now that the nightmares of waking in the night had been exactly that. Stupid alcohol-induced dreams of walls that could talk and broken clocks that still managed to tell the time. There was only one thing to be done. It was pointless sitting in that musty room for another three hours. It was time to hit the road. Get this trip back on track after so much lost time. If I left now, I could eat up the 44 miles to Berwick and be there by midday. I jumped out of the bed and hurried to the bathroom to get washed. It was hard not to laugh, there were no motorcycle boots outside the room next door and the towels in the bathroom were a dirty grey colour rather than the faded yellow and blue of my dreams.

Within half an hour I was packed and ready to leave. I crept down the stairs while Ettrick House still slept although I assumed Catherine Houghton and her son would soon be waking. At least they would have one fried breakfast less to make. I had carefully rolled up £200 in banknotes with an elastic band I found in the haunted chest of drawers, but I needed a pen and paper. The money would more than cover the cost of my overnight stay as well as pay Barry for getting my bike back on the road. It felt wrong just to leave the money without thanking them. I imagined the disappointment in Cathy's eyes as she realised one of her customers had left without saying a word. God knows, she had enough problems to deal with, a son who wore dresses and walls that talked to the guests. Now before you raise your eyes and give me a lecture about being politically correct, I have nothing against gays or transvestites. But this was a small community. Are you really telling me that the nice people of Selkirk didn't snigger when Mrs. Houghton went shopping with her six-foot son dressed in a mini skirt and wellington boots?

The early morning light was filtering through the heavy curtains on the ground floor, but it was still difficult to see through the gloom as I edged along the hallway. Little ornate wooden signs hung on the doors to each side of me. *Dining Room, Customer Lounge, Ladies Toilet, Laundry Room, Staff Only*, each one felt like a demand rather than an invitation. I plucked for Customer Lounge as it felt like the only notice that gave me permission to pass. *Anyway, surely there would be something I could write with inside.* The door opened with a rusty squeal as I tried to adjust my eyes to the dark. Incredibly a dim glow was emanating from the fireplace on the other side of the room. Just the faintest hint of dying flames but enough to cast a flickering yellow shadow across the still curtained room. It seemed strange that Mrs. Houghton would leave a fire to burn through the night. I doubted that Ettrick House followed many health and safety rules. Maybe the big boy was married to the local hotel inspector as well as the Arrowford Snug barman?

My hand was feeling along the shelf above the fire when I first became aware that something was wrong. As my fingers searched for a pen to write with, they knocked over one of the countless dusty ornaments hiding in the gloom. It dropped with a crash and splintered into pieces on the floor in front of the fire. *Jesus Christ, Grant, you idiot. You will wake the whole place up you clumsy oaf.* It was only as I bent down to look at the pieces of broken crockery that it dawned on me; I was not the only one in the room. A chair sat near the fire but far enough away to be hidden in the shadows. Now the flames seemed to flicker to life and spread their glow a few feet further. I slowly straightened up as my eyes turned towards the figure sitting staring at me. Catherine Houghton was motionless in the chair. A thin white nightdress covering her ancient body. Her eyes stared out from beneath the tumbling white hair that cascaded over the old woman's time-worn face. They looked directly at me, but they had no life in them. She said nothing but slowly her gnarled old hand lifted from her side and pointed in my direction. No words came but it didn't matter. I was looking behind her at the massive figure of her son. He stood with his hands on the back of his mother's chair. I could just make out the matching thin white nightdress reflecting in the dim glow of the fire. I reached into my pocket and grabbed the £200 before throwing it on the floor and fleeing.

It felt strange when I burst through the front door to find the world outside bathed in the first warm light of the early morning. I could hear the birds chattering and even the sound of a car passing on the road in front of the building. It all felt so normal. Had I imagined it all? This whole journey had been bizarre, was it me? Cooped up inside looking after Eve all these years. Maybe my head was exploding with the joy of freedom. Did it matter if I was getting confused? Who cared if I was hearing voices in my head? What harm could they do to me? If I was going crazy, then so be it. I felt happy. I felt free.

I found my bike propped up outside the garage that held big Brian's workshop. As promised a new wheel had been fitted. I pushed it through the car park. The large black motorbike still sat beside the car at the front of Ettrick House. At least I had not imagined or dreamed that part of the story. I was laughing as I reached the end of the driveway that merged through a gate onto the country road. A red van was pulling up. A small rotund lady jumped out with a handful of letters.

'Good morning to you. Hitting the road early or escaping without paying?' She chuckled at her joke as she hurried on up towards the house. I nodded and smiled as I jumped on my bike and started peddling towards the little border town of Selkirk. I had barely gone half a mile when the van gave a friendly toot of its horn as it passed me. I pulled up into the side of the hedgerow just as the country road met the busier A 708. It was still quiet except for the chirp of the early morning birds. Despite the rising sun, there was a chill in the air.

I was turning around, cycling back the way I had just come. There was still one last thing to do before I erased Ettrick House from my memory banks forever. I propped the bike against the gate to the drive and walked assuredly back up to the house. I remembered the watering can sitting in the weeds near the garage. My luck was in. The petrol cap on the big shiny black beast was not locked. It sprang open with one touch and I poured the dirty rainwater into the tank. The liquid made a gurgling sound as it disappeared down into the machine. I hurled the watering can back into the weeds and dropped to my knees beside the back tyre. A few turns and the cap came away in my hand. I stayed there listening to the happy chatter of the birds mingled with the hiss of escaping air as the back tyre deflated. A few minutes later and I had completed the same operation on the front wheel. I know you are not going to think kindly of me and maybe you are right. It probably was going a bit too far, but I also managed to pull a few electrical cables out and what also looked like a fuel pipe. Finally, I strolled back down towards my bicycle. It felt good to be even at last with the motorbike world, even if it was the wrong guy. Oh, and the birds were still singing. At least they remained on my side.

Grant

I was always the kind of person who slipped under the radar. Maybe it was because I was not that tall. Most people did not see me as a physical threat and that helped me to get through my teenage life in Glasgow without ever getting into a fight. All around me at school in the seventies and through my early years, I would see boys punching the hell out of each other. Broken bottles and blood being the norm in those days. We thought nothing of it. To me, it was a bit of a spectator sport, like going to a football match but free.

Most of my friend's parents seemed to like me. I think I was considered to be a quiet and sensible young man. My first experience with drugs came when I was sixteen. It was me who introduced them to my group of friends. We had been brought up in one of the more affluent suburbs of Glasgow. I doubt you could have found a less worldly-wise bunch of teenagers if you had tried. At that point few of us had girlfriends. If I am being honest, other than family I don't think I had even spoken to a girl. It was not that I lacked interest in the female sex, it was just that they lacked interest in me.

My father got me a summer job at a small TV training college helping out doing odd jobs. It was 1977 and the engineers and technicians were still caught up in a time warp from the sixties. I became friendly with one of the young workers called Kenny, a long-haired easy-going sort of guy. He asked me to follow him one day up onto the roof of the building during the lunch break. He produced a joint and proceeded to smoke it before offering me a go. I turned him down because I was scared but, in my head, I was already forming a plan.

Three days later as the night descended, I was heading down to Muirend, a suburb of Glasgow on my 50cc Moped. My best mate was riding pillion. Two tough gangsters off to do a drugs deal at a top speed of 20 miles per hour. Kenny had arranged for me to meet his contact Syd the Bin at 10 p.m. that evening under cover of darkness. I had rounded up my friends and told them we could get a lump of hash for £12. We all thought drugs only existed in America or in films. All five handed over their £2 with enthusiasm. Incredibly I had even told my mum about this deal and she laughed. 'It is probably his mother's crushed aspirin he is going to sell you. Don't be so stupid, son. You don't get drugs in Britain.' No wonder we were innocent, I think our parents were even more naïve. Or maybe it was because they spent most of their spare time drinking and never needed to explore the dark underworld of Syd the Bin.

I have to be honest; I was convinced the whole thing had been set up as a joke by Kenny. He did have a cool understated sense of humour. So, we arrived at the dark side street next to Muirend station with little expectation of anyone turning up.

I switched the tiny little engine of the moped off and we sat waiting in silence for the next ten minutes. It was nearly 10:30 when a shadowy figure in a long coat walked over the bridge that crossed the railway. Syd the Bin looked nothing like one of those drug dealers you see in films. He could have been a writer or an artist with his raincoat and trilby hat. I think he was trying to play the part as he hardly looked much older than his two customers.

The next day I met my five mates in the car park of our local shopping centre after it had closed for the day. Incredibly for our £12 we had been given one of those old tobacco tins full of blocks of green cannabis. Even more incredibly we had no idea what to do with it. None of us had even rolled a joint before. So, we stuck little lumps of it into the ends of cigarettes and smoked them. I doubt it had any effect, but we still rolled about the ground going, 'Hey man, I am way stoned.'

I think we sold most of it to other friends but that was the start of drugs for most of us. Smoking hash would become a way of life for many of my peer groups. I never noticed a big connection between dope and hard drugs, at least no more of a connection than alcohol and hard drugs had.

At sixteen we looked far too young to be allowed into pubs. That didn't stop us from trying and occasionally we would be successful. The easiest bar to get into was an old man's drinking den in the city centre. It was also a well know homosexual haunt in those days. Full of old men hiding their sexuality while looking for young guys. Being gay was not fashionable in the seventies, I am not even sure if it was legal. We would drink pints of beer, sometimes bought for us by a friendly customer. The danger point would come near closing time when the group of us would do a runner before we got cornered by the older clientele. As I left one night a middle-aged man came up to me and asked me out. I told him to fuck off, but I also remember feeling sorry for him when I saw the look of hurt on his face. I am sure he would be considered a sexual predator nowadays but, in my mind, he was just some lonely guy looking for someone. So, at sixteen I had been asked out by a man but had yet to speak to a woman.

The closest I came to getting a real Glasgow kicking happened during a bizarre afternoon in a Glasgow boozer. By now I was 18 and this allowed me to drink in heterosexual pubs. By this time, we had purchased 250cc motorbikes capable of doing 100 miles an hour and you still did not need to take a driving test. This crazy law saw one of my friends dead and many of us suffer serious accidents and injuries over the next few years.

I sat with my best mate in our leather biker jackets having a quiet beer in a pub on Sauchiehall Street. The only other customer was a rough-looking guy at the bar drinking his pint. Suddenly the door burst open and Hooley a guy we knew but didn't like walked in. He bought a beer and came over to join the two of us. Now I don't exaggerate, Hooley was a complete pain in the arse. He was a large guy and fancied himself as a bit of a tough guy. I was never convinced though; I think he was just a bully who liked to threaten others. Suddenly there was a loud scream at the bar. I never did find out what the rough-looking guy said to the barmaid, but the reaction from the pub manager and his assistant was way over the top even for the violent seventies. The two of them leapt over the bar and dragged the guy to the ground. One of them then proceeded to smash him in the face with a heavy ceramic ashtray. Now all this would have simply been another spectator sport for us if it had not been for Hooley. He jumped up and danced around the commotion while egging the two attackers to dish out more punishment to the poor guy on the floor. He was also shouting, 'West Coast Angels at the top of his voice.' I think Hooley knew the manager and was trying to make out he was helping them. The guy was finally allowed to stand up and leave. His face was covered in blood and his teeth were smashed to pieces. He left to the words, 'You're barred from this pub for life.'

The commotion ended as though nothing had happened. Ritual violence was just an accepted part of life then. No Police, no ambulances, and no CCTV. I am sure the manager and his staff just went back about their business. Even though I was used to this kind of thing, the brutality of the attack had shocked me and my mate. Hooley sat down again; his big red face full of pride. I looked at him and shook my head.

'What is with all the West Coast Angels crap? You are no more a member of the Hells Angels than I am.'

That taunt was about to come back and bite Hooley and

the rest of us. Thirty minutes later the guy who had been beaten up arrived outside the pub with a bunch of very hard-looking pals as a backup. His beef was not with his assailants, I think he respected them for dishing out such crude punishment. No, it was Hooley they wanted. He stuck his head through the door while making sure he didn't put his feet inside the premises now that he was barred and pointed at our table.

'You West Coast Angels, you are fucking dead. I am outside, and you guys are getting ripped.'

Hooley looked terrified. 'What are we going to do? They will murder us once we leave.' I looked at him with incredulity.

'We! There is no we in this. It is you they want you big stupid moron. Why the hell did you have to get involved?' Unfortunately, it was obvious that the guys outside considered us as being in this together. We sat for the next twenty minutes like three frightened rabbits trapped in the headlights while we tried to think up an escape plan. We finally accepted that our only hope of survival would be to charge the doors and try to make a run for it. Hooley agreed and told us to wait while he did a pee. The minute he went into the gents we put plan B into action. I and my mate simply strolled out and spoke to the gang waiting outside.

'Shocking what happened to you in there big man. You should report it to the Polis (Police). That big guy you are after, we don't know him, but he is still in there.' And amazingly they just nodded and let us go. We walked to the next pub and hid in a corner just in case Hooley made his escape. I doubt he did though. I remember seeing a police car and an ambulance going past sometime later. I never saw Hooley again. I don't think they killed him, but I did hear that he was left in a serious way. I suppose I should have felt bad about leaving him but that is my point. I had earned my survival by staying under the radar. Hooley was still to learn that if you were going to act the tough guy in seventies Glasgow then by heaven you had better know how to handle yourself.

TWEED CONCRETE OVERCOAT

TUESDAY

It was still early in the morning as I cycled through the little town of Selkirk. The large houses and lush green trees gave the place an air of affluence. Like all Scottish border towns, it had lost most of its industrial backbone with the disappearance of the woollen mills. And yet as I rolled along through the deserted streets it seemed as though Selkirk had weathered the storm of change better than its larger neighbours Hawick and Galashiels. I stopped for a few minutes beside a large statue of Sir Walter Scott standing proudly in the town square. A spectacular display of colour spread out around me from the lovingly tended flower beds. My adventure was back on, I felt good. Ok, I was a bit rough from the night before and I could have murdered a coffee, but my spirits soared with every inch of the rising sun.

It was just over 40 miles to Berwick and my evening rendezvous with Robbie. I could easily cover that distance in 5 hours and be at my destination by early afternoon. The

Border countryside ahead was lush and beautiful, there was no need to rush. I reached the outskirts of Selkirk with a slight feeling of disappointment. I had hoped by some miracle to find a coffee shop or even a garage with a coffee machine, but it was still too early, and everywhere was closed. I left the main road on the edge of the town and followed a cycle path sign down a narrow lane. Within a few hundred yards the little road crossed two major rivers. The first was Ettrick Water quickly followed by the better-known River Tweed. It was halfway across the latter bridge that I decided to take another break. The old stone crossing had now been blocked off to motorised traffic and with no other cyclists around I had the view all to myself.

There is something both calming and mesmerising about watching a river flow beneath a bridge. I stood and stared at the dark blue swirling water of the Tweed as it hurried its way towards the distant sea. Even for mid-summer it still looked heavy and swollen, no doubt from the monsoon a few days before. Bits of wood and other debris occasionally floated past, desperately trying to break free from the current and find a hidden refuge. Somewhere they could be free from the endless pull of life. It was one of these that caught my attention. It was too large to be a branch or a piece of rotting timber. Whatever it was, it was heavy. Even the strong current could not bend its slow progress down the middle of the river. The dawning realisation of what it looked like crept up on me. The top part resembled the back of a man's head; the lower part could easily have been a torso. He was clothed in what looked like a tweed jacket. The arms floated out grotesquely from either side as if he was swimming face down.

'A lovely day, have you cycled far?' I nearly jumped into the river I got such a fright. Beside me was a man, middle-aged, well dressed, wearing a deerstalker hat and a tweed suit. Next to him was an energetic border collie that kept trying to jump up on me. I pushed the dog gently away and turned back to look at the river.

'There, something was floating in the water. Look, can you see it?' We both stared at the river in silence for a few seconds. It looked completely normal. Bits of wood, water, and of course no floating bodies. The stranger looked at me and smiled.

'People see all sorts of things in the River. Their imagination can make even the most innocent of things turn into something we dread.' He turned and walked away without another word. The collie following him in that haphazard way that dogs do. Moving from side to side and sniffing everything while keeping their master in view. I stared at the scene for another few minutes. Even though the early morning sun was already beating down, I suddenly felt chilled. *What the hell was wrong with me?* I lifted my bike from the bridge parapet and climbed aboard. Oh boy, did I need that coffee.

After a few miles of twisting and turning on country roads, I found myself once again crossing paths with the busy A7. A modern underpass took me beneath it. Already the sound of traffic could be heard reverberating through the concrete. It always amazes me how the graffiti artist can find a blank canvas even in the remote countryside. The walls of the bridge had been sprayed in a multitude of garish colours. As usual, the words made no sense to me. *Fanboy, CXX, Bones.* Where they names of people or did, they mean something? In my day graffiti had been simpler, maybe even innocent but with a violent undercurrent. *Grant Ramsey gives blow jobs or Govan young team.* Maybe it was Banksy who had dictated that vandalism should go more upmarket.

The thing that makes cycling so much more of a sensory experience than being in a car is the occasional discovery of something magical. It does not happen often. You are usually cursing yourself for buying a bike while you battle up a long steep hill or cursing everyone else in the world while the rain lashes down and vehicles flash by in a cloud of dirty wet spray. The concrete underpass merged into an idyllic little track that ran alongside the River Tweed. On one side of the path stood large bespoke mansion houses surrounded by lush colourful gardens. Each one was a mass of overflowing colour that cascaded out towards me like a silent still fountain. The buildings were done in that mock Tudor design, black stripes running down the face of each wall. Tall romantic chimneys sprouted in groups from the ornate slated roofs. Little twisting paths ran up each of the gardens and disappeared in a sea of flowering bushes and shrubs. On the other side of the track, the Tweed continued serenely on its course. The dark blue water glinting in the sun through the overflowing greenery that ran along its edge. I made a mental note to buy my retirement home here when I won the lottery and cycled on.

I was still in for one final visual delight before my heavenly path ended. A mile or so further on while peddling through the sylvan setting of trees and insects I spied a massive building on the far bank of the river. It was Abbotsford House, the home of the famous early nineteenth-century Scottish novelist Sir Walter Scott. The grand mansion looked resplendent in the distance; a large baronial gothic style building built on the wealth of his well know books. I have to admit, as I peered through the leaves at the distant grandeur, I admired his house more than his writing. My parents forced me to read the classics when I was young, and they bored the pants off me. I know it is terrible to admit but I struggled to read Ivanhoe. The style of early 1800s writing left me cold although I will doff my hat to a great author. When I was ten, I pretended to my mother that I had read it but instead I was stealing quick glances at my father's copy of Lady Chatterley's Lover. Another old classic but this one had naked women in it. Sorry, Sir Walter.

It came as a bit of a shock when my heavenly track suddenly merged with a modern roundabout a few miles later. A large building that looked like a college campus sprawled to my left. Beside it stood a neat little football ground with a sign proudly proclaiming it was the home of Gala Fairydean. Somehow the name of the club fitted perfectly with the idyllic track I had just left behind. Half a mile further on came decision time. A sign pointed right to the ominously named Black Path which was the direction I needed to take. On the left was the lure of the large town of Galashiels. I needed coffee, cake, toast, anything, and everything. I had barely covered a quarter of my day's journey, but my early start had made me very hungry. No, I lie. The overindulgence of beer and nightmares had made me hungry. It was nearing 7:30 in the morning, the cafes and shops would surely be open by now. The decision had never been in doubt. I turned to the left and peddled as only a hungry man can.

It felt unnerving to be back on the main road with cars, vans, and the occasional truck roaring past. The morning rush hour was starting and even a wayside town like Galashiels had its fair share of commuters. I chained my trusty steed to a metal railing outside a glass-fronted coffee shop at the grandly named, Galashiels Transport Interchange. The railing already had one of those cheap mountain bikes leaning against it. It had not been secured, maybe the owner was confident no one would ever want to steal it. The interchange amounted to a small bus terminus opposite a single platform railway station. I watched as an early morning train pulled in from Edinburgh. There were few people on board, but it would be far busier on its return journey. Already a line of city workers was crossing the road to wait for the carriages to come back. I thought about Robbie catching the train from Glasgow to Berwick later in the day on his journey to meet up with me. A thin smile crossed my lips as I imagined his face if I jumped on the train to Edinburgh and surprised him. He would be sitting reading one of his fitness magazines, lost in his thoughts as the train pulled into the capital. I would sneak up behind his seat and scare the living daylights out of him. On second thoughts, forget that. He would turn around, his face red with shock and anger. *Grant, you are so immature, for Christ's sake when are you ever going to grow up?*

The café was fairly busy with travellers waiting to catch a bus or a train. Men in open-neck shirts reading The Times or The Herald. Women wearing summer dresses sitting chatting at one of the tables about the office and who said what to who. A group of young men laughing while trying to catch the eye of the two pretty young girls engrossed in conversation at another table. Everyone looked normal for an early morning. A throng of office workers gathering for a quick coffee before the impending journey. And then there was Maggie. She was sitting at a table on her own beside the large glass front that looked out onto the busy street. She obviously owned the mountain bike parked outside. Now I am not exactly Sherlock Holmes, I deduced this from the fact she was decked out in ill-fitting lycra from head to toe, had a rucksack next to her feet, oh and she was still wearing a cycling helmet. It sat perched on her head like an upturned basket of flowers. She looked comical in a way and she was staring over at me. Maggie had spied a fellow cyclist and she was ready to go for the kill. I took the coffee and cake I had ordered and sat at the only empty table, thankfully the one furthest away from Margaret Lockwood Garrett, or Maggie as I was about to find out.

I know I am coming across as some sort of unfriendly weirdo but hear me out. It would have been fine if it had been a fellow male cyclist. One who would ask man-type questions. Surface talk about different brands of bikes, the weather, how difficult the hills had been that morning. Maggie or females, in general, would delve deeper. Search below the surface and take me to places I did not want to go. They would bring Eve into the conversation. Are you married? do you have any children? Followed by uncomfortable looks of sympathy and concern. I didn't want to be reminded of Eve, our failure to have kids, the spiralling of life down into the depths. In the last few days, I had lost myself in a different world. Soon the reality of the situation would be back, and my escape would all be over.

I made the mistake of looking up and her eyes caught mine. I quickly diverted my gaze back down at the half-eaten carrot cake, but it was too late. I could see her moving in my peripheral vision. Maggie was collecting her stuff together and lifting the coffee cup from the table. There could only be one destination now, and I was the target.

'Hello there. Have you come far? What a lovely day it is. Oh yowsers, did I need a coffee. It's lovely to meet a fellow cyclist.' This was followed by a chuckle as she pulled up the chair opposite me and sat down. Her hand reached out and touched my arm. 'Oh, however so rude of me not to ask first. Is it ok if I join you? I am Margaret, well Margaret Lockwood

Garret to be precise, but please just call me Maggie.' Another chuckle followed.

I soon discovered that Maggie was not so bad after all. She had a habit of asking endless questions but never gave you the time to answer anything before firing in the next statement or question. Oh boy, could she talk though? As I listened to her I could tell that she was an Olympic gold medallist at twittering like a budgie. I soon switched off and became lost in my thoughts as her mouth opened and closed like a rattling machine gun. It was hard to work out how old she was. I suspected she was younger than she looked but the helmet made it difficult to guess. I learned that she was on a three-month cycling holiday around Britain. She had left her home in Bristol two weeks earlier and somehow ended up in Galashiels. Incredibly she had slept some nights outside in fields and forests, only paying for accommodation when nature could not supply it free. Maggie looked like a leftover from the sixties, a hippy, someone who was at one with the land and the stars. Well, that is what I think she told me. I was almost falling asleep by now. The worry was, I had this awful feeling she was going to ask me where I was going and then as she was a wild spirit, offer to accompany me on the journey.

'So, Gary, where are you heading today?' Her fingers touched my arm again as though we were already the closest of friends.

'It's Grant, not Gary. Oh, I need to meet my brother this evening in Berwick. It is a bonding trip, so we are looking forward to spending quality time together on our own.' I sensed Maggie knew I was lying. The word quality and my brother Robbie were not two words that I would ever have put together unless it was an emergency. I was desperately trying to stop my new friend from asking to join me. She chuckled again.

'Sorry Gary, I mean Grant.' Another little laugh followed. 'Well, I have no plans and would be more than happy to join you until you get to Berwick, at least. It would be nice to have someone to chat with.' Now we were both lying, me about my fondness for my brother and her about wanting someone to talk with. Maggie only chatted with herself. She reminded me of some alien creature who had one ear and six mouths. I felt bad as she seemed to be such a nice person, but I needed to be on my own. At least until Robbie turned up. Even though that would probably only last five minutes before we fell out.

'Erm, yes that would be cool. Fine, yes, cool.' I knew I sounded less than convincing but the coward in me did not want to offend her. We both spent the next five minutes finishing our coffee while she talked at me. Eventually, she rose to her feet without missing a word.

'Just give me five minutes to use the bathroom my friend and I'll be back. Don't you go running off without me now, Gary.' She proceeded to remove the flowerpot from her head and take the cycling jacket off while chuckling at her witty remark. I watched her disappear into the bathroom. Maggie looked different without her ill-fitting top and oversized helmet. Her hair was a mix of pink and blonde with dark roots showing through. It looked like it had once been long, but she had taken a pair of sheers to it. It flowed over her head but then ended abruptly when you would have expected it to go down to her waist. She was slim as would be expected of someone who had cycled halfway across the country. I had to admit she was quite attractive for a gold-medal talking hippy. With the flowerpot helmet I had her down as being in her fifties, without it she looked much younger. Maybe early to mid-forties. Like most men, I am hopeless at guessing a woman's age. In the five minutes, she had battered me into submission with her incessant chatter I had grown to quite like her. But that no longer mattered. As soon as she disappeared behind the door marked communal toilet, I intended to put my escape plan into action.

And yet I couldn't do it. I was not sure if it was because I felt bad about hurting her feelings or it was because I am such a coward. I imagined her opening the bathroom door to see me crashing through the crowds in the café, knocking over tables and sending coffee mugs scattering across the floor. She would calmly walk over to the table and shout, 'Gary, Gary, wait for me.'

There was another reason I was not getting the hell out of there. My eyes were drawn to a figure crossing the road towards the café. I could see her through the large glass frontage. Her shape looked familiar although I could not see the face. She was wearing a long raincoat even though it was warm. Her blonde hair was tied up under a headscarf and she had that slow methodical walk of a woman in high heels. Outside the street seemed to empty and dark clouds blotted out the morning sun. The throng inside still chatted and drank their coffee as the figure took each slow step towards the window. She pressed against the glass searching for the person she wanted. I sat frozen to the seat. Terror gripped me as she scanned the inside of the room. It was her face, or should I say lack of face. She looked like one of those mannequins, the contours of her white skin followed the shape of what should have been there but wasn't. No eyes, no nose, no mouth, no ears. Any second now I knew she would find me as I cowered into the seat. The glass was bending inward from the weight of her pushing against it. My hands gripped the empty coffee cup as cold sweat trickled down my back and the words floated into my head. *I am still alive; I am still here.*

'Yowsers that was good. I managed to brush my teeth and get a wash in there. Are you ready to hit the road, Gary?' I turned slowly to look at her, anything to break the inevitable discovery from the thing looking through the glass for me. 'Are you ok, Gary? You look like you just wrestled with a ghost and lost.' I looked back at the window and the sun was shining. The cars were hurtling passed and the Edinburgh train was pulling into the platform opposite. Most of the customers were heading for the door to join the throng already on the platform. I smiled and stood up.

'You know what Maggie? I am glad you are joining me.

I reckon I need a bit of company; it can be lonely on these biking trips.' I touched her arm the way she did with me and turned towards the exit door.

'Oh, and the name is Grant. Grant, not Gary.' She smiled back and bent to pick up her various belongings.

'Well let's get this trip on the road then Grant. After you my friend.'

***

We cycled back along the main road to the junction and the start of the bike route known as the Black path. Maggie had chatted incessantly while riding alongside me. She seemed oblivious to the cars and the danger she was putting herself in. I only half-listened and hardly heard what she said as the busy traffic edged past us. My mind was racing through the events of the last few days. The voice had been there for months but now it had transformed into a shape, a form. Was I being haunted, even being followed by some strange ghost? The whole thing was ridiculous, but something was wrong. I knew what it was but hated the thought of having to confront myself and admit my frailty. The truth was, I was stressed. The last few years of full-time looking after Eve had caught up with me. Yes, I was suffering from Schizophrenia, Paranoia, call it what you want. My head was a mess, but I didn't care. I was already nearly halfway through my week of freedom. Father time was ticking off the seconds and the day of reckoning was advancing towards me like an express train. Fuck the ghosts, to hell with the illusions. I was still free, for now.

We spent the next hour gliding along at a relaxed pace between dedicated cycle tracks and minor roads. Maggie kept me entertained with her machine gun chatter. Some of it I tuned into, a lot I ignored and just nodded my head in agreement. It could have ended in disaster with me insulting her by smiling as she relayed some big mishap in her life. Luckily, I seemed to get away with it or maybe her one ear was deaf. The Black path turned out to be a rather tame track that wound its way out of the edge of Galashiels. Somehow, I had half expected a faceless woman or some irate biker to jump out in front of us. It was hard not to laugh at the thought now that I had Maggie and her flowerpot helmet twittering and laughing beside me.

We arrived on the outskirts of the wonderful little town of Melrose and soon the sight of the famous abbey came into view. I walked my bike over to a low stone wall and surveyed the ruin. It was the opposite of the carefully manicured Abbotsford House. Much of the building was just a shell but somehow it still looked spectacular and sad. A vision of what once was and what could have been. Eve drifted into my thoughts. I was suddenly overcome with a feeling of sadness, as though I might cry. I felt a touch on my arm and turned to look at Maggie. Only it was not her. A burly-looking policeman with a diminutive policewoman beside him stood facing me.

'Good morning, Sir. Come far today have we?' Their sudden appearance out of nowhere had taken me by surprise as I stammered out a reply.

'Not far, about ten miles.' It was the policewoman who spoke next and immediately her tone had me feeling like a criminal. She looked about eighteen, five feet nothing, and was dressed up like an armoured troop carrier.

'And where did you start your ten miles from this morning, sir?'

'Start from?'

'Yes sir, where did you start your journey from this morning. It's not a difficult question.' Before I could reply Maggie decided to come to my rescue, even if I didn't need or want her to.

'Why are you asking officer, I mean is there a problem? I can vouch for my friend Gary here, he has been with me all the time, so I doubt if he has committed any serious crime.' The young woman's face flushed with annoyance. Before things escalated her colleague jumped in with a friendlier tone.

'Could you tell me your full name please Sir? I doubt it is you we are looking for but maybe we could just clear this up and you can be on your way.'

'Grant Ramsey.' He stared at me with a look of confusion for a few seconds before responding.

'Grant? I thought your name was Gary?' I looked at Maggie as she was about to speak and raised my hand to stop her before we both got arrested.

'No, my friend here calls me Gary, that is my nickname. My real name is Grant, Grant Ramsey.' The small unfriendly policewoman gave a smile of satisfaction. I expected her to taser me at any minute. She took out her little notebook and started to read from it.

'Are you the Grant Ramsey who stayed over last night at the Ettrick guest house just outside Selkirk?' I wondered where this was going. My mind flashed back to the vision of Catherine Houghton and her enormous son sitting in the dark. I remembered throwing £200 on the carpet as I fled. It was those two who were weirdos, not me. Why had they reported me to the Police?

'Yes, yes, that's me. I paid before I left, what's wrong?' I could tell the little tyrant in uniform didn't like me. Her reply came with more than a hint of sarcasm.

'Oh, it is nothing to be worried about, sir. One of the guests had their motorbike vandalised during the night. The owner Mrs. Houghton told us you left very early this morning. We just wondered if you might have seen anything?'

Little and Large strolled back to their Police car after a further five minutes of asking questions. I felt they knew it was me who had committed this most serious of crimes but could not prove it. Instead, the delightful little Police lady filled up her notebook as though every answer I gave would be used to send me to the gallows. Her slightly friendlier colleague wished us a happy biking holiday. He looked bored with the whole thing if I am honest. I turned to Maggie and gave an embarrassed laugh.

'Sorry about that, Maggie. Honestly, it was not me. I have no idea what they were talking about. Poor guy, water in his petrol tank, what a shame for him.' She chuckled and gave me a friendly punch on the shoulder.

'I was hoping it was you who had done it, Gary. It would have been hilarious. Anyway, I was more worried they might search us. She was a right stuck up little strumpet.' A puzzled look crossed my face.

'Why would they search us and what would it matter anyway. We haven't done anything wrong.' Maggie placed her hand inside the oversized lycra bike jacket and pulled out a small plastic bag. It was obvious what it contained.

'I was searched near Birmingham and half of my happy stuff was confiscated. Luckily, they didn't find the rest of it. Shall we get going? Your brother might arrive in Berwick before you.' Maggie jumped on her bike while I lifted mine from the stone wall. Melrose Abbey still basked in the sunshine. Pigeons flapped around the crumbling stone walls as a light breeze bent the tall grass to its will. I was laughing. I knew I needed to get rid of her before Robbie turned up but at least she was fun to be around. Anyway, maybe the spooks would leave me alone while I had a companion with me. Even if she did keep fucking calling me Gary.

***

I am sitting on a bench at the two-platform Berwick train station thinking back to the events of the afternoon. Even here at what should be a busy place it feels lonely. Information monitors hang suspended from the roof of the red sandstone building displaying information about trains to distant Edinburgh, York, and London. The eerie silence is broken only by the occasional blur of red and grey carriages flashing past without stopping. It will be another 45 minutes before Robbie's train pulls in. Maybe then more customers will arrive, I need human company. For once in my life, I want to hear the sound of voices, the buzz of normality. I am even looking forward to seeing my young brother again even though I know we will end up arguing. I think I understand what is happening to me, but it does not make it any easier to accept. I am losing my mind. All these years cooped up with my own thoughts looking after Eve has finally caught up. Either that or I genuinely am being haunted. And yet, is that not the same thing? Both conclusions question my sanity.

We left the outskirts of Melrose in the late morning and cycled through rich green farmland along picturesque bike tracks and peaceful minor roads. It became obvious why this route was called the Tweed Cycle Path as the majestic river would occasionally be glimpsed through gaps in the hedges and trees. A stunning old railway viaduct came into view near a place called Drygrange. The modern equivalent of the ancient monument also crossed the river beside it. An ugly plain concrete structure built for function rather than grace. Why is it that the human form loses its beauty with age and yet ancient buildings become more attractive as they grow older?

Somehow by early afternoon, we became lost. Like an idiot, I had followed Maggie as she charged on. I suppose I assumed that if she had made her way hundreds of miles from Bristol then she knew what she was doing. It took us an extra hour to retrace the correct route and from that point on I took the lead. She must have been able to sense that I was annoyed as for once she stopped chattering. I know you are reading this and thinking, poor wee Maggie. Boy, is that Grant guy a bloody moaner. But look, in my defence. I didn't ask her to join me. She just attached herself to the next person she could find, and that was me. So, my mood was not good and then I managed to get two tyre punctures in quick succession.

The first happened as we passed through the centre of Newtown St Boswells. Anywhere with the word Newtown attached to it should be regarded with suspicion. They tend to have those endless box houses packed tightly together, multiple roundabouts, and any shops or amenities are hidden away inside concrete buildings. On top of that, I was forced to repair the first puncture near a bus stop while a gaggle of prospective passengers stood and smirked at my misfortune. I am hopeless at changing tyres. I end up covered in chain oil and can never get the tyre off without ending up in a rage. To add to my frustration Maggie kept talking and trying to tell me what to do.

'Gary, I have a puncture repair outfit. You can patch up that inner tube rather than use your spare.' I looked at her and tried to take a deep breath.

'Look, we are running late after you got us lost. I don't have the patience or the time to mess about with bloody repair kits. Just let me finish this and we can get going. Feel free to press on yourself if you want to.' I think I went too far as she stood there with a hurt look in her eyes and said nothing. It took me almost 45 minutes to get the bike sorted. I knew friends who could do the whole operation in ten minutes. Not me though.

The second puncture occurred just fifteen minutes later as we arrived at a lovely little single-track pedestrian suspension bridge over the River Tweed. This would be my last crossing of the famous water as from now on we would veer North and leave our blue friend behind. Bollards and signs warned us to walk our bikes across. The ornate iron structure looked flimsy as it attempted to stride across the wide river. I cursed and slammed my bike upside down with more than a hint of annoyance. That is the odd thing about bike punctures. You can cycle for hundreds of miles without ever getting one, but you can be sure that when they do happen then they bring their companions with them.

'Just my fucking luck. Another bloody Puncture.' Maggie jumped off her bike and smiled. *Why did nothing ever seem to bother her?*

'Yowzer bad luck Gary. Well, you will have to use the

puncture repair kit this time as you have used up your spare inner tube. Do you want me to fix it for you? I am used to this sort of thing. Here, let me have a look.' My patience was ready to snap. I attempted a deep breath and continued to work.

'Look, Maggie. I am pissed off enough. Can you just leave me to fix this please?' She seemed to take the hint and moved a few steps away before watching me try to take the back wheel off. I wrestled with the mechanism and then cursed loudly as the chain caught my fingers. Suddenly she moved forward and gently pushed me away.

'Let me do this Gary. I am good at this sort of thing.' She was not kidding either. Maggie might have been able to talk for Britain and get us lost with ease, but she was a tyre repair expert. I swear to God she had the whole thing done within five minutes, and that included using her bloody repair kit on the inner tube. I suppose I should have been grateful, but my male ego was now pricked and, instead of being happy I remained agitated. She jumped on her bike and started to push away.

'Come on Gary, we have time to make up. Let's jolly well batter on.' I remained standing beside my newly repaired bike.

'I tell you what Maggie. Give me five minutes. I am going to wash my hands down at the river. You go on and I will catch up.' She stopped and turned to look at me.

'It's ok I'll wait.'

'Look, Maggie. Do me a favour. You go on ahead and I will follow you in ten minutes once this is fixed.' She looked hurt.

'You promise Gary?' I nodded my head and started to walk down the riverbank to the water.

'And my name is not Gary, it's Grant.' I shouted the last bit, but I could already see her crossing the bridge above me. Hopefully, she could not hear the anger in my voice. I was already working out a plan to take a different route in the hope I would lose her. I know, I know. I really am an ungrateful bastard at times. I just can't help it.

I remember letting the cold-water wash over my hands as I hung over the edge of the embankment. The minutes passed, maybe I was just trying to waste time and make sure my unwanted friend would keep on going without me. It must have been at least half an hour before I finally stood up and climbed my way back up to the bridge. Everything seemed normal, the blue water flowed down below, the birds flew between the tall trees on either side of the bank, and no cars or humans invaded the tranquillity. I walked the bike past the bollards and took my first steps to cross. It was at that point that I looked up and saw the figure. She was standing at the opposite end. Perfectly still just looking in my direction. At first, I thought it was Maggie and I felt oddly pleased but as I squinted my eyes, I knew It could not be her. The figure was familiar, we had met before. We both stood watching each other from our respective ends of the bridge, separated by a few hundred yards. I waited for the inevitable movement and watched in terror as it started. Each slow methodical step bringing whatever it was closer to me. I did not want to hear the words again; the truth hurts too much. I would love to be able to tell you that I stood up to it, faced my demons down, and stopped running from my tormentor. But, I didn't. Instead, I fled like a coward into the dense trees and hid away like a frightened rabbit. Eventually, silence descended, even the river became quiet as the warm sun beating through the leaves washed over me. I dare not move in case it found me and eventually I drifted into a tormented sleep of nightmares and visions of faceless ghosts.

I woke with a start and fumbled for the watch under my biking jacket. Nearly an hour had passed since I had hidden in the trees. Something was moving through the forest, looking for me. The sound of twigs snapping as it came towards me. The crunch of feet on the thickly scattered bracken edging ever closer.

'Grant, Grant, what the hell are you doing in here.' I looked at Maggie with her ill-fitting clothes and ridiculous helmet and wanted to hug her. It would have sounded crazy to tell her why I was hiding, so I said the first thing that came into my head.

'Oh, great to see you. I, I just suddenly felt tired and came in here for a rest. I must have fallen asleep.' Even as the words came out, I could feel my face redden. The excuse sounded ridiculous and I could sense the mood of the woman standing in front of me change.

She looked at me and slowly that friendly smile that Maggie wore with ease started to disappear from her face.

She nodded her head as though she finally understood what was going on.

'I see, I see, Grant. It's obvious that you're trying to get rid of me, I get it. I only came back because I was worried something might have happened to you.' She turned to walk away and suddenly I no longer wanted her to leave.

'No, Maggie, That's not true. Wait for me. At least we can make it to Berwick together.' She stopped and looked back. I could see tears in her eyes and now I felt bad.

'You didn't want me to come with you today, it has been obvious. It's my fault, I was just lonely that's all. You are a decent man Grant, enjoy your time with your brother.'

She walked away without saying another word. I watched her disappear into the trees and cursed myself for being such a fool. At least she had finally called me by my real name. I always felt that she called me Gary because she enjoyed the joke.

Eve

We had only been together for about three months when it first occurred. I had organised a break in the Lake District as our initial holiday together. By now Eve was staying every weekend at my flat in Glasgow and then returning home to the place she shared with her sister during the week. Those first months had passed quickly when we were together and then dragged when we were apart. The intensity of being in love can be both beautiful and stressful. I worried unnecessarily that Eve might suddenly change her mind about me. Each hour she was not around would find the voices in my head doubting my ability to hold on to her. She just seemed too good to be true.

We had booked into a little hotel on the edge of Lake Windemere. I could hardly afford it, but it did not matter. The credit cards would continue to build up their invisible threat until the day of reckoning arrived. I remember the happiness that radiated from her as she floated around the room looking in awe at the curtains, the bed, the television, the pictures of flowers that adorned the walls, and most of all the glorious view of the lake that shimmered in the sun outside our window.

I was lying on the large double bed flicking through a

magazine when she started to put on her coat and move towards the door.

'Eve, where are you going?' She gave me that look I would come to understand as the years passed. The one that meant, *why do you ask? Surely you already know.*

'I'm off to the shops. There are loads of little gift places, I'll be in heaven.' She smiled and opened the door as if she had to leave before I could ask anything else.

'Give me five minutes, I'll come with you.' I was not getting five of anything, she already had her feet in the landing outside our room as she replied with a distant smile.

'No, Grant. A woman needs to shop on her own. I will only be half an hour. Read your magazine and I'll be back soon my love.' The door closed and she was gone.

And so, would start the first of the catalogue of odd events that would pepper our relationship until I learned to accept it rather than understand. For the first hour, I continually looked at my watch while my senses searched desperately for any sound of her returning. After an hour and a half, I could stand it no longer and I put on my coat to go and find her. It was a fairly large village but most of the shops were centred on the one side of a long street. These were mainly small outlets designed to cater to tourists. The real shops such as the newsagents and the butcher tended to be down the side streets. She had to be on the main thoroughfare, so I went in search through each one in turn. It took me an hour of pushing through crowds and fending off odd looks as I walked in and then straight back out again.

It was still early enough in the year for the light to fade in the evening. She had left just before three and it was now approaching six o'clock. The sun was still casting a late orange glow that tells you the cold is descending. I was pacing around the room. Should I go back out and search for one last time or maybe report her missing to the local police station? Remember, this was 1989, no phones and women disappearing or being murdered was not uncommon. And yet, Eve had only been gone for three hours. I envisioned the sergeant at the desk looking at me and smirking.

'Look, son. You are in love. Once you are married then three hours without the misses will feel like a dream come true.'

It was the clock face in the room that filed itself away into my memory banks. I would look at many more throughout our relationship as she suddenly re-appeared back into my life. It now showed 6:35, and she had been gone for more than three and a half hours when the door opened, and in walked Eve. She carried a large gift bag in each hand, flowers poked out of the top of one of them. Her face beamed with contented happiness.

Eve sat on the edge of the bed with tears running slowly down her cheeks. I felt like the worst person in the world. I was the one apologising and that was the way it would always be. She gave no explanation as to why she had been away for so long. It seemed inconceivable that anyone could spend so much time in such a small row of shops. And why had I not been able to find her? Look I am not an idiot. I know women can lose themselves when shopping. I convinced myself that it was me who was being unreasonable. In the years ahead as these things happened more often, I would come to understand and even accept the pattern. I pulled her close to me and could smell the sweet aroma of her hair close to my face. We said nothing, it was pointless. I had just arrived at the early stage of understanding that Eve only floated across this world. On the bed behind the two entwined lovers sat various presents. A ceramic model of the village, a book about hill climbing in the Lake District, a box of hand-made chocolates wrapped in a blue ribbon, a woollen scarf, and a pose of little red roses. Every one of them for me. Each one grasped from the place I would never get to know.

PORCELAIN

TUESDAY EVENING

I watched as he stepped from the carriage while trying to manoeuvre his bike onto the platform. Within seconds the brightly uniformed attendant was signalling for the doors to be closed. The impressive-looking train would continue its journey south towards London. Not so long ago we used to compare our railways to the sleek silver bullets of Japan and laugh. Not anymore. The engineering marvel accelerating away from me looked modern and sophisticated. Which is more than I can say for Robbie. He waved in my direction as he wheeled his bike towards me. A picture of gormless clumsiness with a rucksack.

It might have felt better if we had been meeting in the morning and setting off on our travels. At least that way we would not have needed to say much, just follow each other while keeping the required distance. Now we would have to spend the first hours together, eating, and having a beer before one of us made the excuse of needing an early night. You see, that was the problem. I love my young brother; well I think I do? Yes, yes, I do but let me be honest, I don't like him, and I am willing to bet you a fiver that he can't stand the sight of me either.

'So, you did it then, the whole 100 miles? I bet you just got an earlier train and waited on the platform for me to arrive.' He smirked nervously at his little joke.'

'I cycled the lot, Robbie. It is you who got the train and missed half the week out, you bloody wimp.' This was not a good start. Already the sharp comments disguised as jokes had begun. I took the rucksack from him as he carried his bike towards the stairs at the end of the platform. Only two people had left the train, Robbie and a woman who brushed past the two of us as we climbed up to the street that fronted the station. I glanced up at her as she climbed the stairs and then quickly lowered my eyes back to the ground. It was her, she was wearing the same raincoat, the same headscarf tied tightly around her head while her heels clicked against the floor of the metal walkway. *Ignore her Grant, she only exists in your mind. Pull yourself together man.*

An hour later we sat facing each other in the almost empty but aptly named Nags Head on Berwick High Street. Of course, Robbie had insisted that he needed a shower and time to unpack when we booked into the hotel. I was sure he only did these things to annoy me. The quicker we got drunk and had the inevitable fall out, the better. It would clear the air; we could get some sleep and cycle tomorrow in silence while we both sulked.

'So, this Barry guy was wearing a dress!!' Robbie said the words with an exaggerated drawl to make it obvious that he didn't believe me. I don't suppose I could blame him. I thought it best not to mention the motorbike and the other weird things that had happened to me, but big Barry and his frock were too good to leave out.

'Yes, but that's not all. The big guy and his mother Cathie were sitting in the dark at five in the morning. He with her tiny dress on and big wellington boots. It fair freaked me out, I can tell you.' Robbie had that look on his face. The one where he made me feel as though I was half crazy. I wanted to punch him on the nose but instead changed the subject. The explosion would have to wait until the alcohol took effect and tore down the boundaries.

'So, how are Mandy and the boys? How old are they now? Has Scott started secondary school yet?' Robbie sighed and took a long gulp from his beer. I felt like calling him Professor Robbie he was so bloody smug.

'Scott has been at secondary for over four years, Grant. He will be leaving for university this summer. And, before you ask, Brogan-McKay already has his master's degree and is doing well as a project manager in the pharmaceutical industry. Mandy told me to say hello and to give Eve a hug from us all when you get back home.' I shrugged.

'How time flies. I suppose the years tend to drift by when you are stuck in the house day in, day out looking after someone who can't do anything for themself.' He leaned forward and patted my arm.

'I know Grant, I know. Of course, it can't be easy for you, we understand that. But sometimes you make me feel as though your situation is my fault the way you constantly snap at me.' I decided to change the subject before we ended up rolling about on the floor. How the hell did he expect me to feel? His perfect life, kids at university, and the freedom to do whatever he wanted. Jesus, he could have joined me three days ago but even that was too much to ask. Both he and Mandy adored Eve, but in recent years they had backed away. I suppose I blamed them for abandoning her. Maybe the reality was they found it difficult to visit the ghost of someone they once knew.

'Anyway, I am not fucking kidding. I swear to God he was wearing the shortest dress ever. That is a sight I never want to see again.' Unfortunately, Doctor Robbie was on a roll now. He leaned forward with that mock concerned look on his face. The one he usually gave me when a lecture was coming. *How the hell was I going to survive four days of this?*

'Grant, are you still taking the stuff the doctor gave you? You know it's important. Please tell me you are sticking with the medication.' My mind was drifting off as I answered without taking in what he was saying.

'Are you still hearing things in your house? You know the voices you told me about last time.' His mouth was moving but I could no longer understand the words he said. I thought about Maggie. Why had I been so cruel to her? I had talked my brother into joining me halfway through this trip and now I no longer wanted him with me. I could have bypassed Berwick, left him standing in the station confused and alone. I should have continued the journey with Maggie. At least she cared or seemed to care.

'Grant, Grant. Jesus Christ, are you sure you are taking your pills? You are not even listening to me.' I was listening. I was just filtering out his crap. I wished I had found out what Maggie's story was. I had not even asked her if she was married or had children. I suppose I should have been thinking about Eve, not some woman I hardly knew. But that was the thing, I knew Maggie better than the person who used to be Eve. I was left caring for the memory of someone who had left me years ago. Even the cat gave me more affection and feedback. I had my own body and another lifeless one to look after. They both needed to be fed, washed, clothed, moved around, and cared for. I sighed and picked up the two empty glasses.

'Another beer, Robbie? Let's get drunk, it will make things easier for the two of us.'

***

Robbie stood in the kitchen methodically checking through the list of things he needed to place into the rucksack. Each item lay carefully placed on the large dining table. A spare inner tube, tools for a mechanical emergency, a flask, extra clothing, and more. Mandy watched him as she leaned against the fridge, a look of concern on her face.

'It's only three or four days. Surely the two of you can behave yourselves for that time. Just relax and enjoy it.' Robbie looked at his wife and sighed.

'I don't want to go Mandy. It's as simple as that. I don't get on with Grant at the best of times but lately, lately, he just seems to be getting worse. He was always a cantankerous sod at the best of times but now, he has become impossible.' Mandy edged over towards her husband and touched his arm.

'I know my love. I know. You are right, he is not easy to be with, but you have to give him some slack. What has happened to Eve is just so awful. The poor man has been through hell.' Robbie could feel the despair and anger rising inside him.

'I understand all that. Jesus Christ, have I not tried to help over the years? We have all been through hell with this, not just him, you, me, the boys, everyone in the family has suffered. It bloody well helped to see my mum off. The whole thing has been a nightmare in our lives.'

'That's not fair Robbie. You can't blame Grant for your mother's passing. She was unwell even without all the stress of Eve's illness.' Robbie continued to pack his gear. He suddenly stopped and looked at his wife.

'I don't want to go on this trip Mand. I've got a bad feeling about the whole thing. Grant has been getting worse lately. The last time I went around to his place just a few weeks ago he kept me standing at the front door. I reckon he is not taking his tablets anymore. He has been hearing those voices again.' Mandy sighed and walked over to pick up her car keys.

'Just get the trip over with honey and do your best. I spoke to Kate last week and she told me that when she last saw Eve, she was shocked at how quickly the poor soul is deteriorating. Maybe once it is all over then we can try to get Grant back to the psychiatrist.' Robbie continued to pack his bag with a look of resignation. He looked up at his wife and sighed.

'Mand, will you do me a favour while I am away?'

'Yes, what is it?'

'Could you go around to Grant's place? Speak to Kate. Maybe she would know what is going on with him. It would give you a chance to see Eve yourself. Go visit her while he is away, and you have the chance.' His wife tried to smile. It was meant to reassure him but neither of them felt convinced.

'Ok, my love. Of course, I will. Let's get you to the station before you miss the bloody train and give the two of you something else to fall out about.' Robbie pulled the rucksack over his shoulders and followed his wife to the door.

'Will you call me tomorrow? Let me know if you learn anything when you speak to Kate.'

***

It had all started so well. Ok, maybe I exaggerate a bit but for the first few hours both me and Robbie attempted to try and get along. At one point he even told a joke and I laughed. I would repeat it here, but I've forgotten the punch line already. Something to do with Sherlock Holmes and Lemon entry. We left the Nags Head around 8:30 pm and went in search of something to eat. The town was quiet, even though it was midsummer. Maybe all the party animals took a Tuesday off before starting the weekend early the following day. We eventually settled for a table in a small Indian restaurant. A couple were just leaving as we arrived. We took their place as the only customers. Robbie looked through the menu while I pondered if I should have another beer. That was the problem, I knew he would give me a lecture about feeling fresh for our journey the next day. Mr. Perfect only ever had two beers and the occasional sherry at Christmas.

'I am going to have another beer, Robbie. I take it you are not going to start moaning at me?' He looked up from the menu, his reading glasses perched on the end of his nose.

'Yes, let's get a beer and a bottle of wine to share. We might as well enjoy ourselves. We can always head back to the hotel after this and sleep it off.'

I had to admit I was taken aback by this turn of events. Credit where it is due though, at least he was trying. We polished off the curry, wine, and beer and continued to act like two brothers who got along for once. It was now 10 pm, and I was enjoying the evening. We settled the bill and staggered out into the warm air. The streetlights were glowing as a few shadowy figures and the occasional car ambled along the

High Street.

'Well Robbie, that was a good evening. I think this must be the first time we have been together since 1972 and not ended up fighting.' He looked at me and smiled.

'Let's go for a nightcap. Another beer eh? We might as well go back to the Nags Head, at least we know it will be easy to get served.' So that is what we did. Only the nightcap turned out to be several nightcaps.

When we walked back through the doors of the Pub it came as a shock to find the place much busier. Men lined the bar talking and drinking in that annoying way that makes it almost impossible to find a space and get served. Couples and loud groups of friends sat at the tables in animated conversation. I squeezed between two giants at the bar and tried to attract the attention of one of the busy staff. 'Two pints of lager please?' By some miracle, he noticed me and started pouring the beer.

'Busy place. We were only here a few hours ago and the pub was empty.' The barman looked up while the glass he was holding continued to fill.

'Yes, this place has a license until midnight during the week. The only late pub in town. Great for you guys and not so good for me.'

And that is how the two of us ended up getting so drunk. We found a table in the corner and sat talking about mum and dad, school, and the old days. The two of us laughing and comfortable with one another as the beer flowed, reflecting on some of the scrapes we had experienced together when we were kids. I never mentioned Eve once and he refrained from trying to tell me how to live my life. What a pity things had to change so quickly, but then with us two it always did.

It was really going great until I saw the woman sitting with her back to me at the bar. She was perched on one of those tall stools, her legs just managing to reach the floor. Even though it was summer she still wore the raincoat and I was sure I recognised the scarf on her head. It had to be her, why else was she sitting alone? Nursing a glass of gin while everyone around her chatted and laughed. It was as though she did not exist, but I knew she did. My tormentor was back but this time I was not going to let her get away.

'Grant, do you remember that time we let dad's tyres down and he blamed the boy next door?' Robbie was laughing. When I didn't respond he looked at me.

'You ok, Grant?' I could not take my eyes off her. 'What's wrong?' That look that Robbie gave me when he thought I was losing it crossed his face.

'That woman, the one sitting over at the bar with her back to us. Can you see her?' Robbie shrugged and strained his eyes before replying.

'Yes, yes I see her. The woman with the raincoat. Maybe she is expecting it to rain in here.' Robbie laughed at his joke; he had a habit of doing that. My tormentor was moving her arms to lift herself from the seat. She picked up the glass and emptied the contents down her throat before jumping down from the stool and heading towards the door.

'So, she does exist after all.' I was already rising from my seat. At first, Robbie looked surprised, but this was quickly followed by a look of horror. I was running now, trying to push myself through the crowd as the back of the raincoat disappeared through the exit. Robbie tried to make one last grab for me and missed, sending my half-full pint glass tumbling across the floor.

'For fuck sake Grant, stop, stop. Come back, you crazy idiot.' It was too late. I was already crashing out onto the street. It was now dark, and a light summer rain was falling giving the road an orange sheen from the glow of the streetlamps. She was only a few yards in front of me as I reached out to grab her. The faceless lady was already turning around to look at her pursuer.

It was an old woman and she started screaming. Luckily, I quickly came to my senses and stopped before I touched her. She was not even wearing a headscarf; it was just grey hair plastered tightly to her skull. Her blotched red face was lined with age and the effects of drinking.

'Oh my God, sorry, so sorry. I thought you were someone I knew?' Robbie had arrived outside along with two other male customers and some of the bar staff. One of them held my arms behind my back as though I was some sort of sexual deviant.

'Jennie, are you ok? Is this guy giving you any trouble? Shall we call the police?' The old woman looked at me and shook her head.

'Naw, I'm ok. This fucking nutjob is the guy with the problem ah reckon. He is just pissed, let him go.'

It took a lot of explaining and pleading from Robbie before they did allow us to leave. I stood there like a drunken idiot while he told them I had recently had a nervous breakdown and thought the old lady was my wife. When he said the last bit, the barman looked at me incredulously and laughed.

'What, he thought old Jennie was his wife!! Christ that is some breakdown.'

We walked back along the high street to our accommodation for the night. I don't think I have ever seen Robbie so angry and that is saying something when you consider how much I have pissed him off over the years.

'What the hell were you thinking, Grant? Jesus Christ man we could have both ended up in jail. Are you fucking insane? She was an old woman; you could have been charged with assault or sexually molesting her. Oh Jesus, what if my work found out about it.' In my drunken stupor, I tried to make light of the situation.

'Sorry, Robbie old boy. I was just trying to ask her for a date. You know how things are with Eve these days. She doesn't say or do much and old Jennie was giving me the eye.' My poor attempt at humour failed drastically as Robbie exploded.

'You stupid useless selfish bastard. Stop making Eve the excuse for your pathetic behaviour, Grant. You are losing it, completely losing all sense of reality. You've stopped taking the tablets they prescribed, haven't you?' He grabbed me by the lapels of my jacket and pinned me to the wall. 'Go on, tell me you are no longer taking them you crazy fucking madman?'

Unfortunately, things went rather downhill after that. I know you are thinking, how the hell can it get any worse, but it did. I swung a punch at him and got a shock as it connected with his nose. The next minute he was on his knees holding his face while blood poured down his cheeks. I think I was more shocked than him. I don't think I had ever punched someone in the face before.

'Jeez Robbie, I am sorry man. Please forgive me?' I bent down to try and lift him from the damp pavement. The rain was coming down in one of those summer smears that soaks you to the bone. The water was dripping down his face, but I could still see the tears falling from his eyes.

***

I can vaguely recollect Robbie pushing me away and storming off on his own. I knew even in my drunken state that I would have a lot of apologising to do in the morning. What an absolute mess, yet again. It was after midnight when I staggered back into the hotel. The lights still shone in the hall, but all was quiet. No doubt the staff and the guests were all asleep. Not me, I could not face going back to my room alone and I needed another drink. My luck was in. The guest lounge had one of those little coffee machines as well as a small glass-fronted cooler sitting on top of a table near the window. A hand-written notice stated,

PLEASE HELP YOURSELF.
COFFEE AND TEA ARE FREE.

Below this was a list of prices for alcoholic and soft drinks. I assumed this meant my particular beverage of choice would need to be paid for. I helped myself to a bottle of beer and sat down on the flower-patterned sofa. The room looked like something from the seventies. A large mirror stood over the empty fireplace while copious ornaments filled every available space. On a table next to me sat various brochures with over-enthusiastic statements plastered across the front. *20 Exciting things to do in Berwick upon Tweed, Framlington mini zoo with real sheep*, or for those looking for a real thrill, *Lamberton woollen hat museum*.

I stayed there alone drinking beer and thinking about the situation I had somehow got myself into. Robbie was right, my life was a mess. I was completely screwed up, I knew that. The frightening thing was, despite what my brother thought, I was still taking the medication the doctors had prescribed for me. Maybe I should have told him, tried to reassure the poor soul but what was the point? The voices in my head were still talking to me and now things had progressed to another level. I was seeing people that did not exist, except in my sick mind.

I decided I would tell him everything tomorrow. Spill the

beans on all that was happening. Let him help me when we got home. I could go back to see the specialist and maybe get stronger medication. Anything to get Robbie back on my side. It was time to grab his offer of help. Time to listen to what everyone was telling me. Yes, tomorrow I would at long last confide in my brother. I still had four days left before I needed to go back to my life of looking after Eve. The woman I think I still loved. Robbie could take care of me for the rest of the bike run. If he was around and I stayed away from drinking, then we could maybe make it together. Just the two of us, brothers in arms.

I looked at my watch and was shocked to see it was now 2:30 in the morning. I emptied another bottle of beer and staggered up the stairs to my room. My brother was in number 7 opposite mine. I wanted to knock on the door, wake him up and tell him I was sorry, tell him I loved him. I thought better of it and pushed the key into room 6. Tiredness was overwhelming me. I could not even switch the light on or take off my clothes before crashing onto the bed. This is the point where things became weird and confused.

Someone was already in the bed. *Jesus, this must be the wrong room. Oh fuck, I am big in trouble this time.* And yet, I knew this was my room, it had to be. I distinctly remembered the keys with 6 and 7 being placed on the counter when we booked in. Fear and confusion gripped me but maybe the alcohol clouded my senses and gave me the courage I didn't have. In the darkness, my hand reached out and touched the face of whoever was in the bed with me. It was smooth. The contours of the skin were all in the right place but there was no life. No eyes, no mouth. I could feel its arms moving in the dark, coming towards my face now. The hands were cold and hard, like porcelain. We both explored, felt, touched, looking for signs of life. The hands moved down my face towards my throat and then gripped. Tight, so tight, threatening to squeeze the air from my lungs. The face moved to within inches of mine, no breath just emptiness.

'I don't want to die. Don't leave me. I am still here, still alive. I don't want to go, not yet. Please, I am not ready.' The words were spoken softly again. The way a lover would talk. Words of affection, words of something that once was. I was choking, the grip was draining the last air from my lungs. I screamed and fell into the deep black cavern, the same one that the creature beside me had crept out of.

***

I swear to God, that phone will be the death of me. It was missing again. I definitely remembered looking at the time last night when I drank the beers in the guest lounge. *Yes, that's it. I must have left it there. I can get it later. Maybe someone has already handed it in.*

I remember reading once that the more you drink the less impact you feel in the morning. I suppose there must be some truth in that. A stinking hangover is often the cure to stop you from doing it again the next day. The worry was, I had woken on the floor of the room, and other than a desperate need for a drink of water, my head felt ok. Maybe I was still drunk? I have to admit, once again I had overdone it. I stood up and looked at the bed. The light was flooding in through the thin curtains. The covers and pillows lay scattered across the floor. It looked like the world wrestling championships had taken place in my room last night. Of course, there was no sign of the porcelain woman. I shook my head and looked around for something to tell me the time. Not a bloody thing, no clock, no radio, nothing. Except for the tv. I switched it on and the presenters on breakfast tv were talking about some ice-skating dance show that had finished at the weekend. The world was probably about to implode through global warming but don't worry, some no-name had danced around a frozen pond without falling over.

Jesus in a handbasket, 9:15!

Robbie was going to be in an even worse mood now. Before we fell out last night, we had agreed to meet for breakfast at 7:30 and hit the road at 9. I dressed quickly and pulled my stuff together. Maybe he had a hangover and was still asleep? No chance. I rattled the door to number 7 but all was silent. The smell of toast and coffee was wafting up from the dining room on the floor below. *First stop, breakfast, and then Robbie to tell him how sorry I was for being such an arse.*

The dining room had obviously been busy earlier but now it held just two couples. By the state of their tables, they were finishing up. All four of them turned to look at me as I walked in. *Why did I feel they already knew me?* The only table that had not been used was over in the far corner next to a window. I pulled up one of the two chairs and peered out through the glass for any sign of my missing brother.

A tall middle-aged man in a knitted jumper and grey trousers came out of a side door and walked over to me. He had a pencil and a small notepad in his hand.

'Good morning, Mr. Ramsey. We finish taking breakfast orders at 9:15 during the week.' He looked at the watch on his wrist before carrying on. It felt more like a lecture than an example of friendly customer service.

'And, it is now 9:35. I can get you tea or coffee and we could do some toast. I am afraid my wife clears the kitchen at twenty past.' I looked up at him and tried to give a smile as a peace offering. It was obvious that he didn't like me, but I was not sure why.

'Coffee and toast would be fine. I am so sorry; I must have overslept. I think I lost my phone last night, so I had no alarm to wake me this morning.' I then tried to make a joke, but it fell flatter than a pancake. 'I think I had one beer too many last night, eh. It must be the sea air here in Berwick, it's gone to my head.' He looked at me without smiling.

'I think the whole hotel knows you were drunk last night, Mr. Ramsey. You were screaming and shouting in your room when you got back. Some of the customers were less than happy and complained this morning.' As he finished the sentence both of the couples who had been finishing breakfast stood up to leave. They passed my table while giving that look you would expect from a schoolteacher after you forgot to do your homework.

'Erm, oh dear, Well I can only apologise. Sorry, what's your name? Has my brother been down for breakfast yet? Robbie, Robbie Ramsey.' His expression didn't change.

'Your brother left early this morning to go back to Glasgow. He gave me this note to pass to you.' Mr. Happy handed me a small white envelope. I took it and tried to smile but I felt like a scolded schoolboy sitting there while he towered over me.

'I will get you your coffee, Mr. Ramsey. Oh, and you did not leave the money in the honesty box for the beer you consumed in the guest lounge. It is £5 a bottle, so that will be £30.' He started to walk away but then stopped and turned around again as though he had suddenly had a brainwave.

'Oh, and one more thing Mr. Ramsey. You are barred from ever using this establishment again. We run a professional operation here at the Ocean View Guest House. My wife is very upset at your behaviour last night. It has brought on a migraine and she has had to go for a lie-down.' He marched off leaving me feeling like a piece of dirt. I don't suppose I could blame him. It did sound as though I had maybe gone over the top last night. I suddenly remembered my phone. I needed to find it and call Robbie quickly. I would plead, grovel, implore him to come back. Even if he was already on the train to Edinburgh he could always jump off and catch the next one back. He had done this before. Stormed off like a spoilt baby. I would talk him round. I opened the note and read it.

Grant, last night was the final straw. Unless you get help there is no way forward for us to remain in contact. I am not even talking about you punching me or getting drunk out of your face. I am used to that. It has been the way with us for years. It was the screaming like a madman in your room. I knocked on your door at 3 am and you ranted like a lunatic back at me. Some nonsense about a porcelain lady. You made no sense at all. The owner was going to call the police, but you must have finally fallen asleep. Brother, you have problems, big ones and I am not just talking about Eve. Call me once you are ready to take responsibility for your actions. Right now, I am finished with it. I will not expose myself, Mandy, or my family to this madness anymore. I am sorry Grant. I love you as a brother but only you can sort this out. Don't call and try to talk me around. I have blocked your number for now. Oh, and I think my nose might be broken.

I stood up and went out into the hall to collect my rucksack and bike from the storeroom before looking into last night's drinking den or the guest room as it was called. My phone sat on the table. Alongside it stood six empty beer bottles. I could hear Mr. Happy arriving back in the dining room with my coffee. He appeared in the hallway still holding the tray. We eyed each other up as we faced off near the front door.

'I thought you ordered coffee and toast Mr. Ramsey?' I

walked up to within a few feet of him and took out a bundle of notes. I counted out £200 slowly and then placed it on the tray. He looked down and then back up at me without changing his expression of disdain. '£200? It is only £70 for the room and £30 for the beer Mr. Ramsey. That is a total of £100 I believe.' I started to push my bike out of the door with my back to him.

'Keep the extra £100. You can buy your wife a pair of fucking earmuffs for the next time you have a customer that goes over the top and enjoys himself.'

I stood outside the Ocean View Guest House with my trusty companion, my bike. The only friend I had left in the world. The sun was glowing in the sky and the morning bustle of traffic and pedestrians could be heard on the nearby High Street. Seagulls soared overhead while the cool morning air sifted through my bones. It felt good to be alive. No, it felt fantastic to be alive. It was still only Wednesday. I had at least four more days before I had to go back to Glasgow and face the music. I thought about Robbie and tried not to laugh. I no longer needed him. He would be fine, maybe it was better that he had gone, better for him, better for both of us. My hand reached into my pocket for the phone. The screen was blank. The battery had died overnight. I stared at it for a few minutes. It reminded me of Eve. An empty shape without any sign of life. I could see her face reflected in the glass and I knew how much I missed her, how much I needed her to be back in my life. My arm lifted the phone and threw it with force towards the clear blue sky above. It sailed through the air and smashed against the side of the Ocean View Guest House. Now I really was alone. Grant Ramsey versus the rest of the world. I jumped on my bike and laughed as the thrill of being alive washed over me.

Eve

Eve was devastated when we learned we could not have children. I wished it was me who was the problem, somehow, I think we could have both handled the finality of things better. Although we never discussed it, I knew she felt that her purpose in life had diminished. The strange thing was that during the first few years of our marriage I assumed that it would only ever be the two of us. We seemed to drift into this need to have a family and very soon it became all-consuming. Two years of trying and failing followed by tests and then the ultimate disappointment.

The move to the borders and Cairnstone Lodge was driven by Eve. It was probably the only time in our long marriage that she insisted on taking us down a certain path. Years later when I looked back it seemed obvious that she was running away from life. Our friends, siblings, even work colleagues were all producing endless offspring. Every party or family get-together was taken over with talk of wee Johnnie's blue eyes and pictures of cute little Rosie's first tooth. It was ok for me; the men would drift off into inane chat about football or politics. Eve was left with the mothers, the barren lady smiling politely.

The house had been the gate lodge for the long-demolished

Cairnstone Hall. It was very run down having been empty for several years. By this time, I had fallen on my feet as a project manager working in the booming nineties computer industry. Eve no longer needed to work. We could afford the house, we could even cover the massive cost of renovation, none of that was a worry. What concerned me was how remote the place was. The nearest village was miles away and the commute to work would involve a two-hour drive each day. Eve justified it all when she pointed out that I spent a lot of my time either in America or Sweden with my job. *We will still spend the same time together, Grant. I need this place, please just do this one thing for me.* Her unusual enthusiasm convinced me. That was the thing about Eve, it was not that she lacked passion for life. It was just that life was something that happened rather than involved her.

Ultimately the move to the remote Cairnstone Lodge would prove to be a mistake, but not for the first few years. Each time I returned home, be it a day later or after a few weeks abroad, Eve would have added another touch of her personality to the house or the garden. Flowers, pots, windchimes, rainbow colours, cushions, and drapes. We had concluded the major repair work in the first year and after that Eve was able to treat the building as a blank canvas. The problem was we were spending less time seeing family and our friends had all dropped off the radar. Eve still remained close to her sister Kate but even she was visiting less.

I don't blame Eve; it was my fault. I suppose it suited

me to have two lives. One socialising, being the big shot in my work, travelling the world and staying in the best hotels. And when I chose, I could come back to Eve and her magical cottage in the middle of nowhere. What man would not love that kind of freedom? And yet I would convince myself that she was not fading, drifting into her own world. Just a tiny bit more each time I returned.

On one occasion I talked her into the two of us going on a rare night out together. A chance to see other people. Eve reluctantly agreed and we took a taxi into the local village. There was a folk band playing in one of the pubs and before long the drinks were flowing, and people started to dance. Eve suddenly grabbed my arm and attempted to pull me onto the floor. I knew we were both drunk and I flinched at the thought of looking like an idiot in front of the locals. I sat there mesmerised like the rest of the clientele including the band as she stole the floor. There was no ego attached, no look at me, just Eve being Eve. She floated in perfect unison to the guitar, the swinging violin, and the beat of the drums. Her red dress and long black hair shimmering as she glided around us all. It was a night that will remain with me forever. It was a typical Eve thing to do. She could charm both men and women without doing a thing. The only one who was not enchanted with Eve was Eve herself.

I am sure it was only the following week that the real problem started to take bigger steps as it crept into our lives. I returned home from work one evening and the house was silent. This was not unusual, she would either be working in the garden or lost in a painting or making yet another flower basket up. I made myself a coffee and then went looking for her. It was only when I reached the bathroom and found it locked that it suddenly dawned on me that something was wrong. I shouted her name in a panic, but my voice was met with complete silence. It took me ten minutes to find the axe and burst the door down. Eve was laying in the bath. The water had turned cold and she was blue. The frightening thing was she was still lucid and staring sideways at me as I ran over. I was sure she even smiled. The ambulance took almost an hour to reach the house. By then I had already decided that we needed to return to the city and normality.

WOODEN HEART

The house looked like any other you might find in the suburbs of the border city of Carlisle. A middle-class semi-detached red brick box that was built in the seventies. Just another one of the faceless small buildings lined up along the quiet back streets. The garden was tidy rather than spectacular as if the owners did just enough to keep the neighbours happy. The tiles on the front step were cracked and the paintwork on the garage was beginning to fade. At the back of the building, a slabbed path dissected the slightly overgrown lawn. It led to a dilapidated wooden shed nestling under a large birch tree. But It is not the house, the garden, or the little outbuilding that matters to our story, it is what is inside the shed. Nestled amongst the tins, dried-up paintbrushes, and rusty tools is a bike. Not an expensive bike, not even a new one. It is a cheap mountain bike, the kind someone might buy in a burst of enthusiasm and then forget about. But this little machine was about to become a star.

Debbie Blackwood stood in the kitchen. A pan was boiling away on the stove, the steam rising slowly up to the ceiling before evaporating. She watched the egg timer like a robot, no emotion just the same repetitive actions she had gone through almost every day for the last 25 years. It all had to be done exactly how he demanded, eggs soft but not runny, toast well browned but not burnt, and the butter spread evenly over the whole surface of the bread. Any deviation from the ritual would invoke mental torture. Vincent Blackwood was a master of the cutting remark. In their quarter of a century of marriage, he had never physically hurt his wife. In some ways, she wondered if that might have been easier. Instead, he used words to attack. Sentences that could eat away at your soul, burn off any last remnants of self-respect until eventually you no longer existed. You were simply a robot, there to serve him. Your only reason for being alive was to keep him from losing his temper.

It had not always been this way. In the beginning, he had at least made some effort. Debbie was his second marriage. Her friends and family had warned her it would not work. She had only been 20 when they met, he was more than double her age. As the years wore on the gap had become more noticeable. Vincent felt and looked older. Her youth became a threat to him, and his bitterness turned to jealousy and then control. When Debbie had found part-time jobs in a shop or a café his constant put-downs had forced her to leave. Even though the money would have helped, the only way he could handle things was to keep her at home. They rarely went out together and if they did, she had to make sure she looked shabby and remained subservient. If someone gave her any attention, then all hell would break loose once they got home.

The only person who still visited them was Vincent's son from his first marriage. Ewan had struggled with drug addiction all his life. His rare appearances usually coincided with him needing money or a bed for the night. Often, he would sleep rough out on the streets. And yet, Debbie liked Ewan. He would take her side against Vincent and somehow his father seemed to be a bit afraid of him. Ewan or Moonie as he was called by people who knew him would often sit and chat with her when Vincent was out. They would laugh together in the kitchen while Moonie rolled one of his endless joints. The last few times he had visited she had accepted his offer to try one and had enjoyed the feeling of being stoned. It took her back to her college days, the times before she met the man who now owned her. Moonie had last stayed with them just a few months back. He looked thin and emaciated; the hard-living had finally caught up with him. His face was that of a man of sixty and yet he was still only in his forties. He left one morning telling her he would be back later. He never returned and Debbie had a feeling something had happened to him. There was no point in asking Vincent. Even the mention of Moonie would cause him to fly off into a rage.

Her life was now one of trying unsuccessfully to keep her husband happy while making her existence at least bearable. The few female friends she dared to keep in clandestine contact with would often ask why she did not leave him? The answer was easy. He held control of the purse strings, everything including the house was in his name. How do you walk out when you have nothing? Where could she go if she had no close family or friends willing to help her? But then one day, she found something that would change everything.

He was back. Vincent would go to the bookies for a couple of hours each day. She longed for the moment he would disappear out of the door with a copy of The Racing Post under his arm. His mood on return would usually be measured by how successful his bets had been. These two hours would be heaven for Debbie. The only time she would be free from the cloud of dark despair that overshadowed her life.

'Hi Vince, did you have better luck today?' She said the words without even the vaguest hint of emotion. He threw his newspaper onto the table and sat down.

'Are those eggs not ready yet? Jesus Christ woman. I come back at the same time every day. Is it too hard for you to get something right? You have to be the most disorganised person I've ever met. And no, I bloody well did not do better. Stop asking such stupid questions on something you know nothing about.' Vincent was a big man. He liked his food and expected his wife to supply it to order at exactly the same time each day. Three bacon rolls for breakfast, and four boiled eggs on toast at 2 p.m. on returning from the bookies. A three-course evening meal, usually steak or pork chops, and a supper of cheese on toast washed down with four bottles of beer. Add to this his liking for snacks in between meals and it was not hard to see why he was so large and unhealthy. Vincent had suffered from angina for several years but despite the warnings, he carried on regardless. They made a strange couple the seventy-year-old mountain of blubber and the 46-year-old dowdy but slim attractive woman.

He continued to wolf down his lunch while Debbie pretended to keep busy in the kitchen. Vincent became irritated with her if she wasn't active and doing housework. Even though he had stopped her from getting a job he still accused Debbie of being lazy. *I had to work on the railway all those years while you loafed around painting your nails and watching tv.* The reality had been different. His job had mostly involved him sitting around and doing very little. He had been the union man, the one who held the power. His way with words kept him free from ever having to do any real graft. The position gave him influence over both the management and his fellow workers. Now in retirement, he had simply migrated his control from the workplace to his home.

'Where the hell are those jump leads, I asked you to find yesterday woman. The battery in the car was flat again this morning. I had to get Eric at the bookies to give me a jump start. If you had done as I asked and found the bloody leads, I could have used them instead.' Debbie lifted the teapot and started to refill his cup.

'Maybe you should think about replacing the battery, Vincent. It sounds like it might not be holding its charge anymore.' He slammed the newspaper down on the table.

'I will bloody well decide when I need a new battery.

You have no idea what you are talking about. I don't have money to burn you, stupid woman. God almighty it costs enough to keep you here sitting around doing nothing all day.' She walked back and placed the kettle on the stove without replying. Debbie knew it was not worth saying anything. It would just escalate into him becoming ever more vindictive. He suddenly stood up, his jowly face red with rage.

'I might as well find the bloody things myself you useless waste of space. I bet they are in the garden shed. They must be, not seen them for years.' He eased his massive frame up off the chair and went to walk out of the back door. But she stood in front of him. Panic in her eyes.

'No, it's ok Vincent. I should have done as you asked. I'll go and check the shed. You eat your lunch; you've earned it.' He sat back down without protesting. His hand reached for a piece of toast and he dipped it into his boiled egg before placing it into his mouth. Yellow yoke oozed down the side of his cheek as Debbie disappeared out of the back door.

The jump leads he was looking for were not in the shed. She knew it would be a wasted journey. He had probably given them to someone or thrown them out years ago. They both knew damn well they would not be found but he had to play out the game of control anyway. Once it was agreed that the leads no longer existed then he could blame her, the same way he blamed her for every wrong in his life. No matter how minuscule or unimportant it was. Debbie had only walked down to the shed to make sure he would not discover the bike.

He had not been in the back garden for years. She was the one who cut the grass and looked after any manual tasks while he lazed in front of the tv or read the paper.

Debbie stared at the bike with a feeling of pride and excitement. It had only cost £80. Moonie had found it for her. He had even brought it around and helped her hide it from Vincent. He reckoned it was worth double the price she paid as he told her he had got it from a friend. That first day she kept sneaking out to the shed to look it over, her hands almost caressing the faded paintwork on the frame. It was the first thing she had owned in years. Something that had been paid for with her own hard-earned money.

There was a small worn bike bag attached to the underneath of the saddle. Inside she had found a scrunched-up piece of paper with the words Lyoncross Wood written on it. The letters were uneven almost as though they had been scrawled by a child or someone in a real hurry. At night she would dream of the mythical forest and fantasize about finding where it was one day. The cycling clothes that lay on the shelf had either been obtained for nothing or a few pounds from the charity shop. Vincent only gave her the exact same housekeeping money each week. She had to justify every penny she spent. But with some creative accounting and by re-using old receipts she had managed to put by £100 over the last year. Just enough to purchase the bike and clothes. Debbie had even managed to get out and cycle for an hour every few days while he was at the bookies. It was risky and discovery would have ended in disaster, but the sense of freedom she enjoyed had been overwhelming. The little machine was hers; she loved every inch of it. It made her feel free, it made her feel human again.

***

Debbie looked at the packet of bacon and added the figures up in her head. The other food in the bargain bin was no good to her but this would net an extra £2 to the money she was putting aside to buy a bike helmet. Who cared if the meat would be out of date by the time, she cooked it for him. *Maybe with a bit of luck, he would choke on it.* She laughed and placed the packet into her shopping basket.

She walked with a spring in her step back to the house, his house. She thought of the shed and the bike sitting there waiting for her. Maybe tomorrow she would risk taking it out while he was at the bookies. Debbie hated herself for not hating Vincent the way she should have. It was simply that he did not exist to her. She went through the motions but now she lived in a parallel world. He had long ago killed any feelings she had for him or for anything. The bike though had taken her back to a time when she was young. A time when she had the future at her feet. A woman ready to take on the world, before she had met him. He had been older, even handsome at that time, and of course, he had a way with words. The very thing that would first of all attract, then trap, and finally destroy her personality.

Call it a woman's instinct but as she approached the bottom of the street, Debbie knew something was wrong. When the car came into view parked on the drive to the house a deep sense of dread overwhelmed her. *He never came back early from the bookies, what had happened?* The front door was not locked. She walked inside and called his name. When no answer came, she knew the game was up. He was standing in the garden, his face red with rage. Sweat was pouring down his face from both the burning sun and the white-hot anger coursing through his veins. The bike was on the grass beside him along with the lycra jacket and other bike clothes. She stood framed in the doorway, too afraid to speak or move. His eyes bulged in their sockets as his mouth opened to spill out hatred and vitriol.

'You stupid greedy fucking bitch. Where the hell did you get the money to buy this thing? You have sponged off me for the last time woman. Answer me, where did you get it from?' Debbie could not speak. It didn't matter what she said now, it would all lead to the same conclusion. He kicked the bike and sent it sliding across the grass. He was moving towards her now, a gigantic ball of utter rage. She feared for her life, he had never been violent before but this time it felt different.

'I saved the money by serving you out-of-date food, Vincent. You are so fat and greedy you never even noticed the difference anyway.' His face turned purple. She had never spoken back to him. He was just a few feet away from her as he raised his big powerful arm ready to smash his fist into her face. She stood frozen watching him as though it was a play and she was part of the audience. Vincent had turned a ghastly white colour now. He started to fall, his legs crumbling away from under him. He was gasping for breath, trying to speak but the words for once remained in his throat. Sweat dripped down his forehead as he fell to his knees. He was trying to say something, it sounded like 'ambulance', but Debbie was not part of the act, she was just watching. It was not her responsibility to become involved with one of the cast. His torso finally arched forward and collapsed head down onto the slabs of the path with a sickening thud.

She remained where she was for a further ten minutes listening to his irregular breathing until it finally stopped. At last, when all became silent, she walked out into the garden. Debbie picked up the bike and checked it over. It was a relief that it had not been damaged. It would have broken her heart if he had ruined her pride and joy. She replaced it carefully back into the shed and then sat down on the grass. It was time to try and work out a plan of how to get this mountain of dead blubber back into the house before someone noticed what had happened.

***

It was dark before Debbie finally managed to get the body into the kitchen. By using a concoction of bed sheets and ropes she had pulled and pushed Vincent inch by inch towards the house. She then covered him with a large sheet and left the body lying on the floor. By some miracle, none of the neighbours had seen her. The uncut hedges and overgrown shrubs had helped but she knew she had been lucky not to be noticed. The next few days were spent trying to get as much money together as she could lay her hands on. The tin he kept his betting money in had produced £75 but the real bonus had been his bank card. Debbie didn't know the PIN but had found a scrap of paper in his wallet with a few different numbers written on it. It was on the third attempt that it was finally accepted. She was stunned to see that Vincent had over £20,000 in his bank account. A new bike helmet and other gear were purchased and finally, she was ready. Two days after Vincent had dropped dead in the garden, she was ready to escape.

Debbie wheeled the bike out of the shed and placed the rucksack on the path beside it. The sun was shining adding to her sense of elation and excitement. She went back into the kitchen and made a last cup of tea before sitting down in his chair at the small dining table. Debbie stared at the massive body hidden under the sheet and smiled. Suddenly there was a knock on the front door. She recoiled in horror at the thought of her escape plan being thwarted and waited in silence while praying whoever it was would leave. The bell went again and then a minute later once more. Debbie had no choice but to go and answer to see who the persistent intruder was.

A small man with thinning grey hair and a pair of glasses perched on the end of his nose stood on the step. Debbie had never met him before but then her circle of acquaintances was non-existent anyway. 'Hello, what can I do for you? The man looked at her in surprise as though he had not expected a woman to answer the door.

'Erm, yes hi. My name is Eric, I erm know the chap who lives here, Vincent. Are, erm, are you his daughter?' The question may have sounded rude, but the poor man looked confused and slightly in awe of the woman standing in front of him.

'Hello, I am Debbie, Debbie Blackwood, Vincent's wife.' The man's face went beetroot red as he stammered a reply.

'Oh, oh, ok. Vincent never mentioned he was married. We all thought, well…' He was almost choking on the words.

'Well he is married, so now you know. Can I help you with anything?' The little grey-haired man finally managed to pull himself together.

'Yes. It's just that Vinnie has not been to Clark's for a few days. It is so unlike him, we just wondered if something was up with him?' It suddenly dawned on Debbie that Clark's was the betting shop her husband used. She had to think quickly on her feet or disaster might strike.'

'Oh yes, Vinnie is fine. He has a terrible cold and you probably know that he does not keep the best of health. It's his heart you see. The doctor visited this morning and he has told him to rest up for a few weeks. Poor soul, he won't know what to do with himself. Vinnie so enjoys keeping active working on the house and the garden.' Eric raised his eyebrows in surprise before replying.

'Oh well, Mrs. Blackwood. Tell Vinnie that the lads in the bookies miss him and hopefully we will see him again soon.'

Debbie returned to the kitchen and sat back down again opposite the body of her husband. She lifted the cup of tea and took a slow drink before placing it calmly back down on the table.

'Well, Vincent. That was a close shave. It seems the boys at the betting shop are missing you. How strange that they care more for you than I do. They didn't even know you had a wife.' She was chuckling now. The thought of Vincent looking after himself was ridiculous and yet he had kept their marriage a secret as though he was ashamed of her.

'Did I tell you I am going to Scotland? Yes, me and my bike. We are going to find Lyoncross Wood together. I want to thank you for allowing me to go on holiday and of course for being so generous. I won't be back so you can have the whole place to yourself. Oh, and did I mention I changed my name? I am now Margaret Lockwood Garret, but you can call me Maggie if you want. Rather a posh name don't you think. I cycled all the way from Bristol, been on the road for weeks. Free as a bird Vincent. I would love to say I hate you, but the odd thing is I don't. You see you just don't exist, and it's not possible to hate someone who is not here.'

Maggie finished her tea and stood up. She was just about

to leave the house when something crossed her mind. She turned and walked up the stairs to the room that Moonie slept in on one of his infrequent visits. She would usually clean it after he had gone again but this time, she had left it as he had told her he would be back. The room was a mess and smelled of stale cigarette ash and old clothes. In the corner was the decrepit sports bag that Moonie would always arrive with. The fact that it was still in the room proved that he had intended to return. She emptied the contents onto the bed. Dirty clothes, used needles, and other drug paraphernalia lay scattered in front of her. It was the old tobacco tin that she was looking for. It sat in the middle of the pile. Maggie opened it and took out two of the little plastic bags of grass. She placed one in each pocket before carefully putting the tin back inside the sports bag and walking back down the stairs.

Grant

My father was in my life for the first 40 years but not really a part of it. Don't get me wrong, he was not a bad guy. It is just that I have very few memories of him ever really taking much interest in me when I was a kid. My parents worked hard and gradually we migrated from the sixties working class into the growing cult of the seventies middle class. I had a far closer relationship with my mother and a big sister, who I adored, than I ever had with my father.

I can only really recall a couple of instances when I and my dad spent any real-time together. Once was when my mother talked him into taking me to my first ever football match. It was 1968, I would have been 8. We lived in Kilmarnock on the outskirts of Glasgow at the time and the home team where playing Hibs from Edinburgh. I was so excited and looked forward to it all week. Not because I was that bothered about the football, it was more to do with having a real dad for the day. Even if it was just for a few hours, it was still me and him together. Like everything he did with me as a child the day ended in disappointment. I could tell he didn't want to go and as we walked down the road into the town, I could hear the sound of the crowd soaring through the air. We arrived half an hour after kick-off and left with twenty minutes to go. Barely an hour together with my dad looking bored stiff.

The second time was the one that really sticks in my memory. It was 1970 and my parents took me, my big sister, and two younger sisters on holiday to Spain. My dad drove there and back in some old rust bucket of a car. He and my mother argued the whole time while the four of us sat crushed together on the back seat. We camped in a tent each night until we arrived at a hired apartment. Each evening my parents would disappear off to the pub leaving us to look after ourselves. My youngest sister would have only been two at the time. Don't get me wrong, I am not complaining, it was a fantastic experience and my parents were only doing what most parents did in the seventies. They left their kids in the house and went out partying. They would bring us a packet of crisps back though, well my mum would.

Anyway, back to the second time my dad noticed he had a son. One morning while in Spain I went out exploring on my own in the little seaside town of Sant Feliu de Guixols. Even though it was by then a tourist town, the country was still ruled by the dictator Franco and once you hit the backstreets it was another world. Women dressed in black from head to toe would stare at me as though a pasty-faced British kid was something they did not see very often. I bet they miss those days now. On the edge of the town, I found every little boy's dream. Two ancient steam locomotives sat rusting on an isolated piece of railway track inside a small but grand-looking derelict railway station. They looked like dead monuments to a forgotten time. I was able to climb aboard and pretend I was the driver, lost in my own little world. Many years later I read that the line had only been closed two years before and the two locomotives sat alone and rotting into the late seventies.

I was desperate to have a photograph taken with me onboard one of the engines. I was still at primary school and in those more innocent times, a railway engine was something to behold amongst my friends. It seems incredible now that boys would take numbers of steam engines in the sixties as a hobby. Today's kids would stare in disbelief if you asked them to do that nowadays. For one thing, it would require them to look up from their phone as well as use a pencil and notebook.

Getting a photo required talking my father into coming with me to use his camera. I knew there would be no chance of getting him to agree so I used a different tactic. I pleaded with my mother to talk him into taking me for a walk to see the trains. I suppose I could have asked my mum to go with me but, remember this was 1970. Women didn't own camera's and it was a man's job to go out walking. The black-clad Spanish women would have called the police if they had seen my mum tottering along the backstreets in her mini skirt and high heels. Anyway, after much convincing, he eventually agreed, and off we set. I still have the photograph he took 50 years later. It is one of only two photographs I keep in memory of my father even though he is not even in this one. It shows a small but happy kid in shorts smiling while hanging out of the side of the little black steam engine. I was grinning not just because I was on the locomotive, it was also because my dad was with me.

And then an astonishing thing happened. Rather than turn around and go back to the apartment as I had expected, my father asked if I wanted to walk along the deserted railway line to see where it went. I remember the feeling of elation as we trudged along the track through deserted dusty little valleys and grass-grown embankments. Me and my dad, two men together. I felt so grown-up and proud. The walk only lasted for another hour or so until the real reason for our expedition finally transpired. My father found a little bar where we could sit outside in the sun. He was only allowed to go to the pub if he took my mum with him. To be fair, they were only in their early thirties, just kids in some ways. We sat for a few hours while my father ignored me and drank beer with the locals. Sometime later we headed back to the rest of the family. My dad looked at me and said, 'Don't tell your mother that we went to a bar. Just say we walked for hours.' And that was it. For the first ten years of my life, I think I got about three hours of personal time with my dad. It is not a lot in percentage terms, but those few hours are what stick in my memory.

Once I reached my mid-thirties, my father started to change. He was now in his early sixties and had retired. I would watch him in disbelief as he played and relaxed with his grandchildren. It just seemed so strange to see this man who had been such an aloof stranger with his own children suddenly become a loving grandfather. I was still in awe of him and even though I knew he was proud of me; we still only maintained a stiff relationship. And then one day it all changed.

My father never had any interest in football. If I am honest, he never had much interest in anything other than electronic engineering and maths. It was tough trying to have a conversation with him as he would simply turn it towards his work and bore the pants off you. I think that is why he had very few friends. Most of those he did have were because of my mother rather than him.

My partner convinced me to invite my father to travel up to Glasgow to come and watch the wee team I supported. I reluctantly agreed as I knew he would be bored. Memories of that day in 1968 came flooding back to me as we took a train together to the game. And yet, what happened that day was so unexpected. He loved the football match; it was all he would talk about afterwards when we went out for dinner. This is the second treasured picture I keep in memory of my dad. This time we are both in it. Sitting at the restaurant table together. Both of us are smiling, each one looking proud and comfortable with the other.

From that day on he would travel up once a month and come to the games with me. Our relationship flourished as we would go to the pub and talk for hours. I learned things about his childhood that I had never heard before. He would tell me how proud he was of me and wish he had spent more time with me when I was young. Typical of my dad though, this period only lasted for about 18 months before it started to change. This time the rationing of father and son time was not his fault though.

Even though he was now in his late sixties my father was still a fit-looking gentleman. He had been an amateur boxer before he met my mum and was still tall and slim even in his later years. My mother would tell me about the odd things he was doing and at first, we laughed and put it down to him getting older and forgetful. He would do weird things like put his jumper on the wrong way around or place the milk in the oven instead of the fridge. Over the coming months, things became worse. On one of their regular visits to Glasgow, my mum walked into the house ashen-faced. My father had driven through a roundabout the wrong way. After that, he stopped driving and I would go down to bring him up for the football matches. Unfortunately, even that didn't last long as he deteriorated very quickly. By now he would try to get into the car facing the wrong way or my mother would be called by a neighbour reporting my father was wandering around the village like a lost soul. The last time I visited him with my sister's young daughter, she became very upset. *Uncle Grant, why does grandad not know who I am anymore?*

Not long after that, he was placed into care as he became too much for my mother to look after. The last time I saw him he was sitting in a chair staring at the wall. He still looked the same, but he had no idea who I was. I suppose it felt as though I was back to being a child again when I thought he didn't care about me. I am not complaining, my relationship with my father was probably better than many children of my generation. You see, my dad rationed out his time with me. They say quality rather than quantity. That was how it was for me. What little time we had together in a real father and son relationship was what mattered. Alzheimer's is a mean disease; it turns the person into a living ghost of what they could have been. All that potential floats away never to be realised. I still miss him.

CHALK

WEDNESDAY

I found a café on Berwick High Street and managed to have a great vegetarian breakfast without falling out with the owner, fighting with the customers or, being attacked by white ladies staring through the window. I walked to a shop and bought a thing made of paper called a map. People used to use them to plan their routes before satellites or mobile phones were invented. An hour later I parked the bike against the wall of the ancient Berwick Bridge and looked out across the river to the magnificent railway viaduct that spanned the estuary of the River Tweed. For the first time on this trip, it no longer felt as though I was running to a timetable. Now Robbie was gone the shackles were off. It had taken me three days to finally realise that this might be my last ever week of freedom.

There was now no need to cycle a set mileage each day. I didn't even need to make it to any pre-planned destination either. I could go anywhere I wanted to, simply follow wherever the road took me. Even if I ended up halfway down the country,

I could simply get a train back to Glasgow on Saturday. With all that in mind, I unfolded the little map and looked at the names of surrounding towns and villages. I thought Rothbury sounded nice so that was my destination for the day. 50 easy miles through pleasant countryside. I just prayed that my imaginary friend with the porcelain body would not appear today. How could she? The sun was shining, and I felt great.

I cycled for the next few hours in perfect bliss. The route followed minor roads and tracks although occasionally I would cross a busier main road. All around me were large green fields and affluent-looking farmhouses. The River Tweed now flowed to the South but this time it kept its distance and could only be glimpsed through the trees and low hills. Near Gainslaw farm I crossed back into Scotland once more. From here until the little hamlet of Ladykirk, I would remain just inside my home country. The border itself followed the course of the majestic river. The route was busy today with other cyclists. I would pass fellow travellers heading in the opposite direction and wave or smile at them. Somehow, I suppose I just wanted company. It made me feel safer. Ok, I know you are going to accuse me of changing my tune. I meant company I could nod a brisk hello to, not company that was going to give me a hard time and make me feel guilty. I did wonder how Robbie was, and Maggie, and of course I thought about Eve. It was only when her face appeared in my mind that my mood would darken.

The more relaxed timetable allowed me to do a bit of exploring and sightseeing. I had earmarked a disused RAF airfield on the map and decided to check it out. There is something romantic about closed second world war military airports. They conjure up pictures of men with moustaches in flying suits and goggles kissing their sweetheart's goodbye. The heroes walk nonchalantly out to board a Spitfire or a Hurricane and disappear into the clouds never to return. When Eve had been younger and able, we had visited a few of them. It felt as if the ghosts of those who did not come back still lingered in the tall grass that now grew through the concrete. The problem was even though Rendene aerodrome was clearly marked on the map, I could not find it. I peered through hedges and looked around trees, but it still eluded me. A few passing cyclists stopped to ask if I was ok. 'You ok there pal? Is it a puncture? Do you need any help?'

'No, no, it's alright. I am just looking for an old airfield. I don't suppose you know where it is?' My reply would usually be enough for them to give me an odd look and move on. That was the strange thing about cyclists. You would hear them say, *oh you see so much more on a bike than you do in a car.* But that was the problem, they would get on their bike, put their head down and work like a badger to get to their destination. No one seemed to stop and look at anything. They might have well just taken the car. My point was proven by the fact that every time I stopped on this trip another cyclist would come screeching to a halt beside me with a worried expression.

'Are you ok? Have you had an accident? Why are you not moving?'

I had just about given up on finding the elusive airfield

when I noticed a decrepit rusting old gate lying at an angle across an overgrown track. It looked like no one had been down that way for years and of course, I had to give it a try. I lifted the bike over the rotting metal and decided it was best to wheel it along the path. The last thing I wanted was a puncture and other cyclists stopping to ask me what was wrong. The track wound its way through a dense little wood. Bushes closed in from either side as assorted insects fluttered around. All was silent, it felt like I had stepped into a different world.

The remains of the airfield finally came into view just as I was about to abandon my trek along the forgotten track. Like most small airfields the runways of Rendene had been designed into a cross shape to maximise the use of the limited space. The landing strips spread out before me, weed-strewn and overgrown. Bushes and even small trees had broken through the concrete to make the whole place look like something from an apocalyptic film. Any minute now I half expected hungry zombies to appear and take a chunk out of my arm.

On a few of the less damaged areas, it looked as though the local farmer was storing hay. Mounds of tightly wrapped bales stood piled on top of each other. It would have made for a rather depressing vista if it had not been for one thing. My eyes were drawn to the unusual sight of an intact control tower standing near the intersection of the runways. The two-story building looked as though it had been used until relatively recently. The windows still supported glass although many of the panes were broken. I decided I had to explore it even if it meant trespassing.

The inside of the building did not live up to the good impression the outside had given me. The ground floor was being used to store animal feed. Most of the walls had been removed to make the space larger but the stairs up to the next level remained intact. I climbed the wooden steps slowly in case they gave way and emerged into a large open room. Incredibly it still looked relatively untouched. A rotting table with a few broken chairs sat on the floor surrounded by discarded paperwork and smashed bottles. Spread across the rear wall was a large chalkboard that had probably been used to mark-up fights at one time. On either side of it were various faded notices as well as an ancient calendar hanging from a nail. I walked over and flipped through the pages. Pictures of small planes filled each page under the heading, Berwick Flying Club 1972. My eyes wandered over to the board and then stopped dead. In faded letters were the words, EVE WAS HERE. I sat down on one of the old chairs. *Was I never to be free of my guilt haunting me?*

How I wished I still had my phone. I could have taken a picture of the writing, kept it for later to prove I was not insane. The first person I met once back on the road could have vouched for my sanity. *Look, tell me what you see in the picture, tell me it says, EVE WAS HERE.*

Something was moving around on the floor below. My ears could make out the faint rustling of footsteps. As though it was creeping around searching for me. I sat still in the chair not daring to move. It was approaching the stairs now, *oh God! It knows I am here.* The wood creaked and groaned as whatever was coming climbed up towards the second floor. I waited for the white face of the porcelain lady to appear, trapped like a total fool. *Why the hell had I come to this place on my own, what an idiot after all that has happened to me.*

It was an old man wearing a woolly hat. He looked as petrified as me as his head appeared just above the level of the floor.

'Jesus Christ, you scared the bejabbers out of me. What are you doing here? This is private property.'

I spent the next thirty minutes talking to Chris. He owned the nearby farm as well as the remains of the airfield. It was fascinating listening to him talk about the history of the place. He remembered the days when it had been a flying club in the seventies and also had some stories from when it had been an RAF base during the war. His father had even served there having been conscripted before Chris was born. And the best bit? He mentioned that his daughter was called Eve and had often played in this very building when she was a child. It was her who had written the words more than twenty years ago. My sanity was back, and maybe the ghost was gone at last.

***

I was back on my bike and hungry. The stop at the old airfield had taken longer than I had expected. It was time to do a bit of real cycling and charge on to Wooler, my planned lunch stop for the day. Once more I crossed over the magnificent River Tweed on an ancient stone bridge and passed back into England. Another half a mile saw me arrive in the delightful little village of Norham. It was one of those quintessential small English settlements. Neat little rows of houses enclosed a central grassy square with a stone monument shaded by large trees. I had not planned to stop but a metal sign advertising coffee and cake caught my eye. Several cyclists stood talking in groups, a myriad of different bikes lay propped up against the side of a brick wall. Some of them were drinking coffee or water from paper cups.

I found a space and carefully placed my machine in amongst the bikes of my fellow adventurers. Most of the crowd were male although a few females and even children could be spotted amongst the multi-coloured cycling attire. I followed the sign pointing to the takeaway but was dismayed to find myself at the end of a long queue. A feeling of camaraderie could be sensed from the happy chatter and buzz emanating from those in front of me. I tried to work out how long I would have to wait and if it was worth it when a voice, I recognised filtered down towards me from further up the line. It was the word *Yowzers* that had caught my attention. I could see her now, about a dozen people between us in the queue. It was the helmet, the one that looked like a flowerpot. It was still perched on her head and of course, she was talking to whoever was near. The helmet bobbed in unison with each word she spoke.

I waited on the other side of the road and watched. The coffee idea had been abandoned, I wanted to see which way she went as well as to check out if she had hooked up with any other poor soul. Typical of Maggie she arrived holding her coffee and proceeded to talk with just about every other cyclist in the crowd. People would leave and others arrive and yet she still buzzed around chatting. I remained watching until eventually nearly 45 minutes later she lifted her rucksack from a table and climbed on board her old mountain bike. It was hard not to laugh as she set off down the road. Sophisticated-looking cyclists passed her in either direction on expensive bikes wearing high-class gear. Then there was Maggie, she looked like a day-tripper who had found an old bike in a skip, but strangely she seemed happier than any of them.

She was heading South, the very direction I needed to go to get to Wooler, 17 miles further on. Now, I know you are going to think of me as being a complete weirdo. But let's be honest here. My journey and what has been happening to me has hardly been the stuff of a family day out has it? I think I understood my life was disintegrating around me. It helped me not to question some of the decisions and warped logic I was using. Maybe I could have just caught up with her, apologised for being an arsehole and we could have journeyed on together. I think I was frightened that she might tell me to go to hell, or maybe I just wanted company but at a distance. Anyway, weird or not, I decided to follow her but keep out of sight for as long as was possible.

The winding country roads were mostly flat and hemmed in by hedges on either side. Maggie was slow so it became easy to catch up and then stop for a while. A few minutes later I would see her again in the distance. Unfortunately, the sun had taken a rest for the day as the sky darkened. Once again, I cursed myself for being so stupid and throwing my phone away. At least I could have checked the weather and got a heads up that I was about to be soaked. My mind wandered back to that first Sunday, just three days ago and yet it felt like a lifetime had passed since then. The Douglas Inn had been the last time the weather had been really bad. The air now had that heavy feeling as if something spectacular was about to be unleashed on the earth.

It was while passing through the village of Ford that I lost her. The country track crossed over a busy main road before regaining its solitude on the other side. My interest had been peaked by the beautiful stone buildings of the tiny settlement. A sign proclaiming, *Lady Waterford Hall*, stood outside what looked like an ancient school building. I stood there wondering who the venerable lady had been. A large information board nearby would no doubt have told me the story but suddenly I was aware that I might lose track of Maggie. I jumped back on my bike and peddled furiously in the direction I knew she would have to take. There was only one way to go, South. Turning either left or right meant following a busy and dangerous road.

I charged on towards Wooler as the light dimmed and the clouds above became angry looking. The map showed me it was barely ten miles, but the country lanes seemed to double back and turn at odd angles making it feel like I was moving sideways rather than forward. Maybe I was just annoyed with myself for losing Maggie. *Surely, she would end up in Wooler?* There seemed nowhere else to go. In my frustration I became lost. Somehow, I had always found my way to wherever I had planned to get to on this trip but now I was no longer sure. The road met yet another T-junction. No signs gave me any clues whether to go right or left. I could no longer even tell if I was even heading South anymore. I chose left as the first spots of rain started to fall and pulled the bike over to a hedge at the side of the road. It was time to put on my rain jacket even though the air felt oppressive and warm. It was still the lesser of two evils rather than getting soaked.

As I pulled the waterproof awkwardly over my arms the sound of an approaching cyclist filtered into the edge of my hearing. Just the merest rustle of rubber on tarmac approaching me through the swirl of the now increasing rain shower. The sky was a deep black, this was going to get messy. It was her. Even from a distance, I could see Maggie's outline, the shape of her body, and the odd way she cycled. I wanted to embrace her, suddenly I needed another human near me. The road, the rain, the frustration of being lost, and dare I admit it, the fear of being alone had suddenly overwhelmed me. I dropped the bike and walked out into the middle of the lane as she approached. 'Maggie, it's me, it's Grant. Oh God am I glad to see you. I am sorry, really sorry for the way I behaved towards you.'

She pulled the bike up beside me. The gloom surrounding her as she removed the helmet. I stepped closer, just a few feet away, and looked into where the eyes should have been. The face staring back at me was blank, white, and lifeless. Her arms were already moving towards my throat. The rain now fell in a torrent, splashing off the surface of the road, running down my face as her hands touched my neck. Cold steel fingers encircling around my throat. Tenderly at first but then gripping tighter and tighter. I was gasping for breath now as we melted together in the deep wet rain. I wasn't ready to die yet, *who would look after Eve? She still needed me even if the end was coming.* I swung my arm with every last bit of strength I had and felt it float through the air. I was free again. Three steps backwards and I crashed through the hedge and into the watery ditch adjoining the field on the other side. I let the dark take over my soul and remained hidden and alone in my little sanctuary as my body closed down.

***

I was looking at the sky, the sun was shining. It reminded me of one of those dreams where you wake up and for the first few seconds, you're not sure where you are. I was on my back at the side of the road, confusion reigned. A woman was looking down at me, concern in her eyes.

'Gary, Gary, it's me, Maggie, are you ok? What on earth happened?' I sat up and looked around. It was the same road but somehow it looked different. There was still a hedge behind me, but it looked impregnable. No ditch, no rain, just me and the bike laying in the middle of the lane.

Between the two of us, we checked both me and the machine over. Neither was damaged.

'What did you see Maggie, how did you find me?' She laughed and the flowerpot helmet moved in unison with her head.

'I was just coming around the corner and realised it was my old cycling buddy. I recognised you even from a hundred yards away. I shouted, erm, well I shouted Gary and you turned. Next minute you must have hit the grass at the side of the road and over the handlebars, you went you silly sod. I am really sorry, my fault again. You must be growing to dislike me.' I wanted to laugh but still had more questions.

'Was that it, did you not see anything else, anyone else?' She looked at me with a hint of confusion.

'Anyone else? Gary, we are in the middle of nowhere. I was trying to get to Wooler but seemed to have become lost. Oh, there was one thing.'

'What, what, one thing. What is it?'

'Well, you were shouting your head off when I arrived and pulled up beside you. It must have been the shock of the fall. Are you sure you are ok, Gary?'

'What was I shouting, tell me. What was it?'

'You were screaming, *get your fucking hands off me*. For a minute I thought it was me you meant.' Are you sure you are ok, maybe you have concussion? Did you hit your head when you fell?' I sat down again on the grass verge and looked up at her.

'Maggie, can I say sorry and ask you for a big favour?' She took her flowerpot helmet off and shook the badly cropped pink and blonde hair that fell over her face.

'Yes, of course, Gary. What is it?'

'Would you mind if we teamed up for the rest of my bike trip? I mean I am only here until Saturday, but some company would be fun, In fact, no, It's not even that Maggie. I need someone to be with me. Someone to look after me for the next few days. Would you do that for me?' She looked puzzled and reflective. For once she seemed to be lost for words. We looked at each other in silence for a few more seconds. 'Please Maggie.' She nodded her head in agreement and held out her hand to help me to my feet.

'Oh, but if we are to team up Maggie, can I ask you to do one thing?'

'Go on, what is it?'

' Can you call me by my real name? It's Grant, Grant not Gary.' She smiled as we both climbed back onto our bikes.

***

We followed the twisting little country roads for the next hour without meeting another cyclist or pedestrian. A few cars scuttled past until we finally emerged at a junction with a busy two-lane carriageway. My accomplice pointed to some buildings sticking above the trees a mile or so away. 'Yowzers, thank the sweet Lord. That must be Wooler at last, Gary. I told you we would find it.' I looked at her and gave a wry smile.

'Oh yes, Sorry, I meant Grant. Come on, I need a coffee, race you.' With that, she sped off down the busy road as traffic weaved dangerously around her. I shook my head and followed.

We sat on our bikes staring at the stone building and the sign declaring, *Lady Waterford Hall.*

'Are you sure this is not Wooler, Grant? I mean you did have a bad fall. Maybe you hit your head and have concussion but don't realise it.'

'Maggie, for heaven's sake. I do not have concussion and even if I did, we would still be standing in the village of Ford, not Wooler. We must have doubled back. Let's go and find someone who can give us directions. At this rate, we will be lucky to make it to Rothbury by nightfall.'

It took another two hours to navigate the country lanes and finally arrive at the picturesque little market town of Wooler. I reckoned it was only 30 miles from Berwick but with the additional mileage added on we had completed nearer 40. Once again, I had failed to make my planned destination for the day. Rothbury would have to wait. It was mid-afternoon and I felt like settling where I was for the evening. A nice little hotel room, a shower, a few beers, and a restful sleep sounded like perfection to me. Unfortunately, I had not counted my travelling companion Maggie in the equation. 'How about we stay here for the night, get a room in one of the wee hotels?' She looked at me with a worried expression. It suddenly dawned on me what I had just said.

'Oh no, no. That is not what I meant.' I tried to give a jokey laugh, but it came out more like a guilty cough. The fact was the last person I wanted to share a room with was Maggie. It was not that she was unattractive, it was just that, well no, just no.

'I meant we get separate rooms. Hahaha, you thought I meant...' Now it was her who looked uncomfortable.

'Oh, of course, Grant. I know what you meant. Yes, fine, fine. Let's see if we can book in somewhere. I am looking forward to getting a long hot bath and a change of clothes.' The awkward moment had passed but I still sensed something was not quite right about her reaction to us booking rooms for the night. Maybe she had wanted to travel on to Rothbury, who knows? I needed a beer and a rest; she was free to go on if she wanted to. And yet, I was glad. Somehow, I knew my demons might leave me alone if Maggie was around.

We tried every hotel on the main square without any luck. At each one, I would approach the reception with hope in my heart only to be told they were fully booked. Everywhere we went we would see bikes and cars outside warning us that inside was already full. Our search progressed to guest houses, bed and breakfast establishments, anywhere. All full. I was becoming more and more irate while Maggie just seemed to laugh it off. The only time a shadow of disappointment crossed her face was when Mrs. Clotworthy of Station Road Guest House told us we might get a place in the nearby Hightown Caravan Park.

It proved to be another waste of time as once again the falsely over-polite receptionist told us they were fully booked. It was at this point our luck changed. Well, it seemed to. As we pushed our bikes down the road to the exit of the caravan park a man strimming the grass waved to us. He turned the noisy machine off and walked over. He had an odd stoop as he moved as if one half of his body was lower than the other. He lit a cigarette and popped it into what looked like a toothless mouth while he surveyed the two of us for a few seconds.

'Names Ferris. I take it you tryin to get a place for the night? No chance, high summer, and fete on this coming weekend. Always fully booked round these parts.' I nodded to him for supplying such useless information but sensed he had better to come.

'I got a caravan you can have for the night. Not luxury but got water and it's yours if you wants it.' I tried to act cool and not kiss him. Maggie said nothing but she seemed slightly more enthusiastic about a caravan than a hotel.

'That would be great. How much and where is it, my friend?'

'Be usually £50 for the night but this being fete weekend comin, and town bein busy, I spects to gets a bit more.' I knew he was a chancing bastard and that the caravan might not be five-star, but I needed a bed. Who cared what the cost was. I played along with the charade until its inevitable conclusion.

'Ok, I'll give you £70, final offer.' He puffed on the cigarette and smiled. I had been wrong, he had teeth, just two, black ones in the middle of his mouth. Suddenly he turned and started to walk away. 'Hang on, Hang on. Ok, what do you want for the caravan?' He stopped and looked me up and down, then did the same with Maggie.

'Well, I don't know. Not sures if I can trusters you to look after it. £120.'

***

Maggie was a strange woman in many ways. One thing that made her so different from any other female I knew was her discerning eye for luxury, or to be more accurate her lack of care for luxury. Eve would have taken one look at the place and walked back to the car. The caravan that the robbing bastard Ferris had squeezed £120 from me for was an absolute dump. It sat hidden at the bottom of a rutted field near a run-down old cottage. I assumed the building was his but for all I knew, he could have just taken the money and pretended that he owned it. The inside smelled damp and unloved. It still had all the windows intact although green mould had spread over the glass. Incredibly the water still ran in the sink and the shower worked so long as you liked it cold. I looked at Maggie and she laughed.

'This will do fine, Grant. We have our sleeping bags; it is a lovely night. Get that look off your face and start enjoying yourself you old misery.' The words stung. Was I really so miserable? It was ok for her. I am sure her life was perfect. It must be, she was always so cheerful. Maybe Maggie would understand once she learned more about Eve. I threw my rucksack onto one of the grim-looking sofas and we set about making the place habitable.

A few hours later we sat in a bus shelter back in the town devouring fish and chips out of a bag. It was one of the best meals I had eaten in a long time. Life at home was all microwave dinners and cold pasta. There was simply no time for anything else. Looking after Eve was a full-time job even with the help I received. We wolfed down the delicious takeaway with the added bonus it stopped Maggie from chattering for ten minutes. The two of us had buzzed around the caravan getting it cleaned up while she asked me endless questions about my life with Eve. I tried to reciprocate but oddly when it came to talking about herself, she would proclaim there was little to tell. Her devoted husband Ernest had passed away some years ago leaving enough money for Maggie to indulge in a passion for cycling and being outdoors. How I envied the simplicity and freedom she had. It did seem odd that she had such a crap bike though for someone on a three-month trek around Britain.

We finished up our meal and carefully placed the empty cartons into the plastic bin attached to the bus stop. 'Right Maggie, time for a few beers I reckon.'

'Oh, I don't drink, Grant. I might just head back to the caravan and get some rest.' I could not hide my feelings of disappointment. The other thing was, I didn't trust people who did not drink. They were usually bible thumpers or at best boring. That didn't seem like Maggie though, so I tried to talk her into staying with me. Ok, I am not being completely honest with you here. There was another reason I needed her close to me. She was back. The porcelain lady was sitting on a bench a few hundred yards away. The square was busy with tourists and locals milling around in the early evening haze. I knew it was my tormentor, she sat alone facing the buildings on the opposite side of the road. If Maggie stayed close to me, I knew I could stay focused and the ghost of my guilt would keep her distance. I understood now that I was persecuting myself for leaving Eve and that ultimately, I was heading for a nervous breakdown. Maybe the fact that Maggie was with me was now the reason the apparition was here in my head. I would face my demons once I went back home to the woman I still loved, but for now, I needed just another few last days of freedom. Is that so wrong?

'Stop being such a bloody bore, Maggie. Surely you can keep an old friend company while he has a few drinks. You can even call me Gary if you want.' She sighed and then nodded her head in agreement with a rueful smile.

'Ok, it's nice you calling me an old friend even though we hardly know each other. I don't have many people I am close to. Of course; I'll tag along with you. Why not.' The words seemed strange. I had assumed that Maggie would have loads of friends with her easy-going attitude to life.

I know you are probably reading on with the expectation that I made a fool of myself again. Either got into a drunken brawl or fell out with my new pal? No, for once I behaved myself. Maggie would have endless conversations with strangers while I sat lost in my thoughts. Five pints later, well ok, maybe it was six, actually, I think it was seven, we staggered down the road back towards Ferris's luxury caravan. Ok, ok, I staggered while Maggie attempted to keep me walking in a straight line. She even linked arms with me at one stage which I thought was nice. As we left the lights of Wooler behind and headed down the little back lanes I could sense she was following. Every once in a while, I would stop and signal for Maggie to cease talking. We would stand and listen, but all would be silent except for the sounds of night insects and the leaves of the trees fluttering in the breeze.

'Who exactly do you think is following us? I mean it can't be anybody you met tonight because you never spoke to a soul. Jesus Grant, you really are an unsociable bundle of joy.' She said the words without malice and laughed off my concerns as those of a drunken man.

The caravan looked slightly more hospitable as I settled

down on one of the sofas and started to unroll my sleeping bag. In the absence of electricity, Maggie had purchased some scented candles and was now boiling water on the little stove she had produced from her rucksack. This was going to be the awkward bit. The one-bedroom looked damp and dirty; I assumed the best thing would be for each of us to take one of the two sofas in the main room.

'Ok if I have this one Maggie? God, I am done in. It has been a long day.' She handed me a cup of tea in a metal container and lifted her sleeping bag from the remaining sofa.

'If it's ok with you Grant I am going to sleep outside. The night is warm, and the ground will be dry after so long without rain.' I have to admit I felt hurt. I simply wanted to sleep but it felt like I was being accused of having some other motive.

'For fuck sake Maggie, what the hell. Do you think I am going to jump on your bones or something? Get a grip woman and don't be so stupid. For a kick-off, I don't fancy you and for your information, I am married. Maybe things are difficult, but I still love Eve, I always will.' Maggie sat down on the sofa beside me and looked into my face.

'Grant, it is nothing to do with you. I am going to tell you something.' Even though I was drunk my ears pricked up at this.

'Go on Maggie, don't tell me you are actually a man and you had a sex change before you left Bristol?' I knew it was a stupid and probably insensitive joke but, in my defence, seven pints can mess with your reasoning. I took her hand and tried to backtrack. 'Sorry Maggie, that was mean. I know you must miss Ernest. Ok, what is it you want to tell me?' She stood up and lifted her sleeping bag from the sofa before picking up one of the burning candles sitting in an old cup. Her face was lit up by a dancing yellow glow that projected her shadow onto the wall behind. She looked almost ghostlike as she spoke. This time the words sounded, harsh and cold.

'As I said, it is nothing to do with you. I can't sleep inside; I haven't stayed in a hotel since I left home. Each night come rain or shine I stay outside.' She turned and walked out the door before shouting, 'My name is not Maggie, there is no Ernest and I have only come from Carlisle.' The words were hardly out of her mouth before I was grabbing my sleeping bag and following her into the night. This was one story I needed to hear. Oh, and no way was I going to sleep in this caravan on my own. I just knew who would be coming to visit me if I did. I could sense her standing in the dark, unable to come any closer while Maggie was with me. It would wait, as it had done for years. What was another night, another few days, my time was running out. Both of us knew that the clock had been ticking from the day I left. It wanted the whole thing to end sooner. I just wanted to make it to Sunday and my only hope had just walked off into the night holding a candle.

'Maggie, Maggie, wait for me.'

Eve

It was not that it happened overnight. Looking back, I can place it all into little memories and instances that built up gradually as each year passed. Maybe I am even making it sound as though it was always depressing or sad but that would not be true. We still laughed, went out, and enjoyed life as best we could. Once we understood what was happening to Eve, we learned to watch out for the danger points. I tried to stay ahead of the game, but the changes started to happen more frequently. At first, I could see the fear in her eyes but eventually, even that faded away. It was as if each door was closing on her thought processes. Once the key was turned it was gone, only to be held in my memory rather than hers.

One day we sat talking after the carer had left. She was looking through our wedding photographs, she looked beautiful the way she always did to me. We had been having a normal discussion about her day, my job. Sometimes she would get confused, wander off track but I had become an expert at steering her in what could best be described as a haphazard direction. She was looking attentively at the picture of the two of us standing in the garden after the ceremony. I in my suit with a pink rose in the lapel, her in a sparkling off-the-shoulder white dress. The day had been hot and sunny. The flowers and shrubs behind us were a mass of bright colours. Eve looked at me and then back at the picture. She lifted the book and pointed at the photograph.

'Who are these two people. They look so happy; do I know them?'

During the next few months, things deteriorated quickly. I made the decision to take early retirement from my job to look after her. I know now that it was a mistake. I should have paid for help and kept my independence. At first, it was great to have freedom from work and be able to find the time to look after Eve and the house. But as the years passed, I became trapped and resentment kicked in. She deserved her independence as well. Maybe Eve had faded away by then, but small pieces of her still remained even though they became less as time passed. We became like robots, each day going through the same routine, the happy memories falling further and further into the distance. By the end, I no longer knew her, and I am sure she had no idea who the man she lived with was.

Solitude

Even the road is self-isolating. The way the stars have always done

Listen, listen, the world has stopped

It is time itself that separates us, it is time alone that bonds.

We will meet again at journeys end while the clock still ticks

The only difference is we now walk this dusty road alone

Our final destination will never change.

DRESS SENSE

THURSDAY

The cars on Kingstown road were crawling along towards the city centre. This was the main northern artery into Carlisle from the M6 Motorway and traffic was busy throughout the day. It was also 5:30 p.m. and the rush hour was adding to the congestion. Moonie sat on the bus staring out of the window, but he took no interest in the houses passing by. The street his father and Debbie lived on was just two stops away. He hated going back to that place, cap in hand begging for accommodation or money. Moonie would only turn up as a last resort. He had never been close with his father but at least in the early days, they had communicated by shouting and arguing. In the last few decades, his father had given up trying to change his son. Vincent Blackwood had his own demons to fight never mind those of his boy. The two of them accepted each other by avoiding contact even when Moonie came crawling back because he had once again hit rock bottom.

The bus edged up to the stop just outside a large petrol station and Moonie jumped off. He usually tried to time his arrival for around lunchtime when Vincent would be at the bookies. For once his visit would not require him to ask for money from his father. He was here on an errand to pick up something he had left behind on his last trip a few months before. Moonie was looking slightly healthier than he usually did. He was still gaunt and looked more than his age but at least some colour was back in his face and he had added a few pounds to his emaciated skin and bones.

He liked Debbie, mainly because he felt sorry for her. It felt strange to have a stepmother who was the same age as him. Moonie had only been 10 when his real mother had died. Like him, she had her problems with addiction. He knew his father's bitterness came from having a wife and son who cared more for alcohol than him. the real victim was Debbie. Moonie knew she was a kind-hearted and at one time an out-going young woman who had been seduced and then ruined by his father. He had even helped her get that bike she was desperate for. The one they had hidden in the garden shed. Moonie told her it cost him £80 but in reality, he had simply stolen it from one of the neighbour's gardens. It was a win-win as far as he was concerned. She wanted a bike and he needed the money, any money he could get his hands on.

He was approaching the house now. For some reason, he felt more nervous than usual. Maybe it was because it was now early evening and he knew his father would be sitting down to his dinner. It felt strange to intrude on their domesticity even if it was mired in intolerance. He preferred arriving when the old bastard was out. Somehow his father seemed to be slightly afraid of him. As if he looked at his son and realised what he had created. Moonie had expected to return that day after he had last visited. It had come as a bit of a shock to get six weeks in prison. It was not his first stretch, he had done many, but simple possession of class-A did not usually carry a custodial sentence. Maybe the judge was fed up seeing him come through the courts yet again, or as Moonie suspected, the judge was in a bad mood that day.

He rang the doorbell and peered through the dirty glass. Moonie fidgeted with both impatience and nervousness. He intended to say a quick hello to Debbie and then head up to his room. As soon as he found the stash of dope, he had left behind that day he intended to make a quick exit. He tried the bell once more and was surprised when she did not answer. Debbie would never be out at this time and one thing was for sure, neither would his father. This was eating time and he stuck rigidly to his meal schedule. It was the main thing in Vincent's life, that and the bookies. Moonie walked around to the back of the house and tried the rear door. Still no answer. He turned one of the discarded flowerpots upside down and stood on it to peer through the kitchen window. Nothing moved. Finally, he reached into his pocket and took the key in his hand. He would just have to brave it out. If they were in, maybe watching the tv he could quickly nip upstairs, grab his stuff, and be gone.

Moonie stood like a statue in the kitchen staring at the sheet on the floor. He knew exactly who was under it without having to lift it. There was only one thing that could be so big and that was the body of his father. He knew he should have felt some sort of emotion, maybe tears, sadness, anything, but he felt nothing. Well, that is not completely accurate, he did feel one thing. He felt happy, not for himself but for Debbie. He could not help but smile. He knew she would have gone, wrapped the body up, and left it. He also knew that the bike would be away from the shed as well. She had finally made her break for freedom. That was the only slight emotion Moonie had while standing in the presence of his dead father. He was an addict, and his next drink was all that mattered. He did not care about alcohol, it meant nothing to him, the same as his father. He simply had to have it. That and any drugs he could get his hands on, and by whatever means. Moonie was not a bad human being; he was just a human being who had gone bad.

The stench in the kitchen was over-powering. Not only did it reek of fried food, it now had the creeping smell of death to go with it. Moonie shrugged his shoulders and climbed the stairs to the room his father condescendingly let him use on his rare visits back home. He opened the door and immediately his eyes focused on the sports bag laying on the bed. Its contents had been emptied onto the duvet. He threw the bag onto the floor and rummaged through his scattered belongings in a desperate bid to find his stash of drugs. There was no sign of the tin. Moonie cursed, not in anger, more in frustration. He knew Debbie had taken the stuff with her. Why not? She had enjoyed the few times they had shared a joint together. He would have done the same, who could blame her. He had taken her money for the stolen bike, so she had every right to take his hash.

Moonie was about to leave when his eyes caught sight of the bag, he had thrown on the floor. He bent down to pick it up while fully expecting it to be empty. The tin he had been searching for was still inside. Four of the six bags of grass remained along with all of the wraps. If it was possible for him to feel good, feel anything, he did at that moment. Just a fleeting emotion, something that he had long forgotten in his continual quest to feed his addiction. It was not the joy of finding his stash mostly intact, that was just part of his daily routine. Every minute, every second was taken up with finding ways to feed his addiction. He felt nothing at finding the drugs. If the tin had been empty, he would simply have moved on like an automation to seek out another supply and his next fix. No, it was because Debbie had thought about him. She knew he might come back looking for his stuff. She had cared enough to leave most of it still in the tin. He wondered if maybe he should have charged her only £60 for the bike. Moonie sat down on the bed and rolled his sleeve up. He picked up one of the dirty needles from the bed.

The door slammed shut behind him as he walked out

into the garden. The old sports bag was hanging over his shoulder with the tin safely tucked inside. He wanted to get away from the house fast. The last thing he needed was to be caught carrying drugs again. Not only that, they might implicate him in the death of the man lying on the kitchen floor. His mind was racing. *I wonder how long he has been dead. Why did she cover his body up before leaving?* It was only now that the seriousness of what he had found started to make him feel uneasy. Now that he had sorted himself out and found his stuff reality was starting to hit home. Once his father's body was discovered the police would soon find out that he was the last one to visit the house. He disliked the idea of betraying anyone, Debbie, even more so, but he had to think of himself first. There was only one way out of this. Moonie knew he had to hide his stash and then for the first time in his life contact the law. He laughed at the thought of being a model citizen and phoning the police. They would no doubt give him a grilling. but the truth for once was that he was innocent. The body was nothing to do with him, he had simply found it when he returned to collect his clothes. Anyway, he had a solid alibi for once. He had just been released from prison. Even the cops could not get around that one.

***

My eyes opened and at first, confusion reigned. I was looking up at the sky. It was a hazy blue with just the merest hint of clouds scattered through it. The sleeping bag felt damp from the dew rather than the unlikely event it had rained during the night. My back hurt like hell. Sleeping out in the open always sounds great at night when you are drunk. When the morning hits and you wake to cold sobriety and a thumping head things feel a bit different. I could not remember what day it was. *Please don't be Friday or Saturday, that would mean I have to go back. Go home, go back to Eve, and have a life of endless loneliness.* I counted the days, trying to remember each one. Sunday and the Douglas Inn, Monday and big Brian in his mini dress, Tuesday the day I fell out with Robbie, Wednesday the day I teamed up with Maggie again. *Yes, yes, it is only Thursday. I still have a few days to go until Sunday.* As my memory got itself back into some semblance of order, I turned to see the woman sleeping contentedly inside her sleeping bag a few yards away. There was a fold of pink and blonde hair sticking out of the top, yes it was Maggie alright.

But that was the thing. It was not Maggie at all. It was Debbie, she had told me that last night. How ironic I had given her such a hard time for calling me Gary when all along I had been using a name she had made up. The joke was on me. I think the joke was always on me with this strange but lovable woman. She was far smarter than she made out. That was why I found her story so incredible. How had she ended up with a man like him?

I had followed her outside last night as we placed our sleeping bags on a flat patch surrounded by tall grass at the perimeter of the field. The evening was warm and still. She had taken a few old lanterns with candles from the decrepit caravan even though the moon was casting a dim glow over the surrounding trees. Maggie rolled a joint and I smoked my first spliff in decades. For once it felt good to lay there and listen to her talk. Finally, she had something interesting to say as she told me her story. It probably helped that I was stoned though. She talked about Vincent, how she had once loved him but slowly their marriage had crumbled. The endless years of being stuck in the house becoming nothing more than an unpaid servant. Even worse the constant put-downs and chipping away at her self-belief until she became nothing, a robot.

It was at that point that my situation finally hit me, and I fell apart. Maggie had ended up exactly like Eve. A faceless lady made of porcelain. There was no justice, no pattern. It was simply fate. I had given Eve all the love and support I could, but she too had become nothing. A living body with no life. I feel like a fool now remembering how I started crying as she spoke. Maybe my emotions overwhelmed me, and it probably didn't help to be drunk and stoned as well. Maggie was holding me, comforting me. She listened while I told her about my life with Eve. For once she said nothing, she would just occasionally nod her head in sympathy. It felt good to be close to someone, close to a woman again. It had been years since Eve had been able to communicate with me. Sometimes I would hold her close but there was no warmth, no life. I also told Maggie about my week on the bike so far and some of the scrapes I had got into. Of course, I left out any mention of seeing things and strange ladies following me. It was at that point that she took my hand and whispered gently.

'Grant, why do you carry so much guilt? It is not your fault what has happened to Eve, you have done your best for her. You are not to blame, stop beating yourself up. You have done nothing wrong.' Her words took me by surprise. It was as if she knew the demons in my head were haunting me.

When I pulled myself together Maggie told me about the bike she had saved for. How much she had loved her stepson Moonie even though he had wasted his life. And then came the twist in the tale. The part where Vincent had a heart attack and she didn't help him. Now it was her turn to become emotional and my turn to hold her. What a pair we made sitting outside on the grass in the middle of the night. We stayed quiet for while thinking about the situation. I remember the last words we spoke before falling asleep.

'Do you mind if I keep calling you Maggie? It won't feel right changing it to Debbie now.' She wiped the tears from her eyes and laughed.

'From the day I got the bike I was Maggie.' There was a pause before she spoke again. 'Grant, do you think I will go to prison when they find his body? I passed the joint back to her and exhaled. Boy did I feel wrecked. I was probably not the best person to try and be a lawyer and give advice.

'Well, I think you broke the law by not reporting his

death. The thing is though, who is going to know that you didn't try to help him? You could just say you found him dead when you came down the stairs. Honestly, Maggie, I think the best thing you could do is call the police and tell them how he treated you and that was why you just walked out. I reckon any judge will be lenient and no way will you go to prison.' She looked at me with hope in her eyes.

'Do you reckon Grant? And I am sure the few friends I have would back me up. Oh, and Ewan, I mean Moonie as well.'

'Yes, honestly, it will be fine.' She took a long puff of the joint before stubbing the remains out on the grass.

'Ok, I think you're right Grant. But when should I call them? I mean, should I do it in the morning.' Her reply suddenly hit me for what it meant. I would have to go home tomorrow. The minute I was alone she would re-appear and force me to go back. The porcelain lady was waiting for Maggie to go. I edged nearer and put my arms around her. My face buried in the pink and blonde hair.

'It is up to you Maggie. I don't want to go on alone, but it is unfair to ask you to risk running any longer.' She pushed me away gently and looked into my eyes.

'Then it is agreed. We stay together and keep travelling until we part on Saturday. Forget them, the police can wait for me.' We both started laughing, helped by the buzz from the grass we had smoked. Each of us elated at the thought of three more days together as free people. In some ways, both of us were probably going back to some sort of prison.

I vaguely remember drifting off into a peaceful sleep just after Maggie asked me her last question.

'Grant, there is just one thing I want to ask you.'

'Yes, go on, final one as I need to sleep.'

'You know back in the caravan you said I didn't need to worry about your intentions, is that because I am so ugly? You said you don't fancy me.' I sat up again and looked at her.

'Maggie, I said I don't fancy you, that has nothing to do with how you look. You are a beautiful woman both inside and out. Vincent kept you down because he knew someone else would step in and take you from him.'

'Do you really think so?' She had a glint of sadness in her eyes.

'I don't think so, I know so. If I was not married, I would feel differently about you, about us. Can we get some sleep now, I feel totally wrecked?'

'Me too Grant. I am stoned, it's your fault. You are a bad influence on me.' She started chuckling and it was so infectious that it made me follow suit. We lay in the grass like two teenagers and laughed until it hurt and finally sleep took over.

In the trees at the other end of the field, the faceless figure stood hidden in the dark. At the sound of our happiness, it turned and crawled away. It had admitted defeat for now, but it would be back. I knew that.

***

We sat on our bikes at the entrance to the field we had slept in last night. Both of us looked back at the old caravan and then at each other. I think each of us felt that we had just had the high point of our trip. Maybe it was the looming realisation that the week was running out. Journeys end was approaching, responsibility and accountability beckoned. Maggie had wanted to turn left and head back into Scotland. I could sense that she desired to go deeper into the Borders and lose all sight of her home in Carlisle. We compromised and agreed to keep going South until we came to Rothbury. Maybe from there, we could head West towards the mass of Kielder forest and the large man-made lake that surrounded it. I remembered visiting it with Eve many years before. I don't know why but somehow; I had a feeling that we would play out our final battle there.

The 22 miles to the little market town of Rothbury looked like an easy run on the bikes. I reckoned we could do it in less than three hours. Maybe get some lunch and then spend the afternoon and early evening getting as close as we could towards Kielder forest. The sun was shining once more. I knew I had been lucky with the weather on this expedition. All the rain I was due had fallen on that first day. Maggie seemed so much quieter as we peddled along. It was as if she had dropped the pretence of being someone else and was now her natural self.

I followed behind my cycling buddy along the little country lanes. My plan was to keep her in front of me, so I knew she was there. Give me something to focus on so my imagination would not run away with itself. The road rose and fell although few of the hills were particularly difficult. After five days of biking, I had become used to the effort required. Also having a companion with me made the miles feel easier.

We passed a man walking in a field holding what looked like a fishing rod. I assumed the blue Landrover parked at the side of the road nearby belonged to him. When we were young me and Robbie had often gone fishing together. I tried to work out why we had ended up bitter rivals rather than brothers. The wheels of the bike hummed monotonously as they ground along the tarmac. I drifted from thinking about Robbie to wondering how Eve was. *What if something had happened to her while I was on this trip? What an idiot I had been to throw my phone away. Kate might have been trying to call me.* I speeded up and within minutes was beside Maggie. 'Hey, I don't suppose I could borrow your mobile to call home.' She pulled up and we both stopped.

'Why do you want to phone your sister-in-law? I thought you said it was agreed you would make no contact for the week.'

'Yes, I did, but now I think it would be better just to check how things are.'

'Grant, she will be fine. Relax. Anyway, why don't you use your phone?'

'Because I don't have a phone, I threw it away.' Maggie raised her eyebrows at my answer before replying.

'Well, I don't have a phone either. Vincent did not believe

in them. Why don't you try a phone box, there's bound to be one in Rothbury.' With that, she smiled and headed off. I was already changing my mind. She was right. Eve would be fine. If I called now it would only break the spell of freedom I had, and my adventure might be over before I was ready to go back.

We passed through a tiny picturesque village called Ilderton. Stone cottages, a few big houses, and of course a large church. Signs pointed left and right to places called Roseden and Lilburn. This really was idyllic lonely countryside. Occasionally we would pass a group of fellow cyclists but most of the time we glided along in our own little green world. The last few miles into Rothbury proved to be slightly tougher. The fields gave way to small hills and rough scrubland covered in tall trees. It was still a joy to be out though and very soon we found ourselves approaching the town. It looked similar to Wooler only maybe slightly larger. We had reached the point of our journey where decisions had to be made, but not before coffee and lunch. I was starving and my back and shoulder hurt from rough sleeping and falling off bikes, in that order.

We spread the map on the table and sipped our coffee. The café was busy with locals and cyclists, but we had found a table in the corner having chained our bikes up outside. Breakfast consisted of a cheese toasty and cake, perfection on a plate. The journey to Kielder Water and the massive forest would be a long trek. It was now midday and I reckoned it would take us around six hours to get there over some hilly terrain. One thing I had already decided on was no more crap caravans or sleeping rough. Tonight, whether Maggie joined me or not, I intended on bedding down in a good hotel. A bath, nice meal, beers, and hopefully no fucking ghosts. That was the plan anyway, I could always dream.

Suddenly Maggie jabbed her hand onto the map and pointed excitedly. I looked at where the tip of her finger was and read out the words. 'Lyoncross Wood.' It was in the middle of nowhere about five miles from the village of Falstone on the edge of Kielder Dam. This was the place I hoped we could get to and with a bit of luck find some accommodation. I remembered visiting the large man-made lake at Kielder some 30 years ago with Eve. We had stood holding hands while we gazed out into the shimmering blue water. In love with each other and in love with life.

'Maggie, it says Lyoncross Wood. That is the clue. You are pointing at a bunch of trees on a hill.' She laughed and gave me a playful prod in the chest.

'Trust me, Grant. That name, it's the one I found written on a piece of paper when Moonie got me the bike. I always dreamed of finding it and now we have. I reckon it's a sign, that must be where we are destined to finish.' I shook my head and started to fold the map away.

'Let's get one thing straight Maggie. We are staying in a hotel tonight. I am not sleeping in a field or a forest, and certainly not Lyoncross whatever it is called.' She had that uncomfortable frown on her face again. The one whenever I mentioned sleeping indoors.'

'Well, you can go where you want Grant. Anyway, I don't have much money left. Vincent's bank card is not working anymore.' I gave her a concerned look.

'When did you last use it?'

'Oh, it was way back in Galashiels, the day we first met. I've tried it a few times since then and it has been refused. I'll give it another go here. I'm sure we passed a bank machine out on the main road.' I reached out and put my hand over hers.

'Maggie, don't try the card again. I think they might have found Vincent and they will be able to track you through the internet to wherever you are. We still have today and tomorrow free. I will get more money from the cash machine; it will be safer. Then on Saturday, I'll come with you to the police station before I go home.' She slid her fingers into mine.

'Ok, but can we still go to Lyoncross Wood? Please, Grant.' I sighed and then shrugged.

'So long as it has a fucking hotel, I will go wherever you like.'

***

We left the café and unchained our bikes. I asked Maggie to wait down a side road and try to be inconspicuous while I went to find a bank or to be precise a bank machine. The last time I entered one of those buildings Noah was still trying to fill up his Ark. Like everyone else I still complained about them being closed down though. Rothbury High Street had become even busier in the hour or so since we had arrived. Cars lined every available spot on either side of the road. Even the cramped spaces down the middle had been filled with tightly packed vehicles of assorted colours. The pavements buzzed with human traffic. I was desperate to get back out into the solitude and quiet of the green hills and trees. Finding a bank machine proved to be harder than I expected. Like most towns in Britain, Rothbury had succumbed to charity shops and food outlets. Most real shopping was now done in the large superstores on the edge of the settlement.

I eventually spied what I was looking for. Most of the street comprised of two-story dwellings, this one was three stories high. From a distance, I could see the ornate arched windows built into the impressive blonde sandstone building. It had to be a bank. It was no coincidence that even in poorer towns than this one the most affluent-looking structures were always churches or banks. Religion and money seemed to hang together while the rest of the world struggled to survive. My instincts were not wrong. It was a pleasant surprise to find it was even the bank I was with. I placed the card in the machine and typed in the number. Two minutes later I was inside waiting in a small queue. Three times I had attempted to procure my own cash and after refusing me twice the little metal bastard decided to eat my card.

The nice lady behind the glass screen looked me up and down with suspicion. I explained what had happened and asked for £500. It was as though I was asking her to hand over her own money. Eventually, after pressing a few thousand keys she gave me a false smile and placed the banknotes on the counter.

'I must apologise, Mr. Ramsey, I am not sure why they put a hold on your card. That's it cleared now. Have a nice holiday.'

I walked out of the building with my winnings. On the opposite side of the busy road was a green square with a large ornate stone cross. It seemed to be a gathering place for cyclists arriving and leaving the town. A sea of coloured lycra and bike helmets milled around chatting and laughing. It was not them that caught my attention. It was the Police van parked nearby and the four officers wandering amongst the throng. They were obviously on official business, most likely looking for someone and I knew who. I hurried back to the street I had left Maggie down and to my horror discovered she was no longer there. Our bikes were chained to a lamppost but no sign of my erstwhile companion. There was nothing to do but sit it out and hope she had not gone far. She eventually appeared ten minutes later, all smiles and flowerpot helmet. 'Maggie, where the hell have you been? I thought we agreed that you needed to stay in the background until we get out of this place.' She held up a plastic bag and smiled. Almost like a child who had been given a surprise present.

'Calm down Grant, my you are a worrier. I just went to look in one of the charity shops and guess what I bought.'

'I have no idea, a hamster?' She ignored my sarcasm and continued.

'I got a dress. Not worn one for years. Vincent said I looked like a tart in a dress so I wasn't allowed them. And you know the best thing?'

'Go on, tell me. I am all ears.'

'It was an absolute bargain, only 50 pence and still new.' It was hard not to smile. She seemed so happy. It was time to get out of town though and the quicker the better.

We were soon on our way. Unfortunately, the first few miles out of Rothbury required us to traverse a fairly busy road. Cars flashed by in both directions as I kept my cycling partner in sight up ahead. I was desperate to get back onto the cycle tracks and country lanes before someone noticed Maggie. Although I could not be sure I felt certain she was now a wanted woman. Was I being selfish not pushing her to report what had happened to her husband? Yes, I was. I convinced myself that a few more days would not matter. I was sure the authorities would just give her a rap on the knuckles anyway. It was not as though she had a hand in Vincent's death even if she did have a reason for wanting him dead. Anyway, I now knew that without Maggie my freedom was over. Call it what you like, either guilt or insanity but the porcelain lady would swoop the minute I was on my own.

We passed through the village of Thropton and soon found ourselves back in the deep rich countryside. The traffic disappeared but the terrain was becoming more difficult. I felt exhausted and even small hills seemed to take it out of me. In my head, I dreamed about sleeping in a comfortable bed and having a long hot bath.

We came to a bridge that spanned the river Coquet and stopped for a rest. On the other side rose threatening hills bordered by dark conifer forests. We were heading into the vast Northumberland National Park. The sky seemed to be cloudier the further west we moved. The wind was also rising although luckily it was behind us and proving to be a help rather than a hindrance. Maybe my run of sunny weather was coming to an end.

I rested my bike against the wall of the bridge and peered over into the river. It was still attractive but lacked the majesty of the River Tweed. Maggie was already on the other side of the short span and suddenly started climbing over the wall. 'What on earth are you doing now?'

'I am going to fill my water bottle up, won't be two minutes.' I shook my head in disbelief.

'Are you crazy? The water will be dirty, you can't drink that stuff. It's probably full of dead sheep.' My words had no effect on her decision as she continued to scramble down to the water's edge.

'I've been doing this ever since I left Carlisle and it hasn't harmed me so far. Anyway, I have a filtration bottle, it cleans it up.'

'Why not just let me buy you a bottle of water, would that not be easier?' She was already out of hearing range and would have ignored me anyway. I laughed and went back to looking at the river. Just two more days and I would have to go home again. I was lost in my thoughts for a few more minutes and then caught sight of Maggie crouching down on the opposite riverbank. She was kneeling as she reached out into the water to try and fill her water bottle. Something was moving down towards her. My gaze was drawn towards it, at first, I felt confusion, but this quickly turned to horror. The porcelain lady was advancing slowly down the bank towards Maggie. I screamed a warning at the top of my voice, but the sound was lost in the wind and the swirl of the river. Now the figure was only ten yards from her, moving stealthily towards its unsuspecting victim. I was running, running like a madman across the bridge, shouting and screaming. Within seconds I leapt over the wall and was sliding down the riverbank towards the apparition. I could only see my tormentor, her shape now blocked out the view of Maggie leaning into the water. Three more massive strides and my body was in the air hurtling towards the ghost. I collided with a sickening thud and both of us went crashing into the cold river with an almighty splash. But it was not the porcelain lady I had taken with me. It was a stunned woman wearing a flowerpot helmet and holding a water bottle who sank with me into the depths.

I was thrashing about in the ice-cold water in a blind panic when I felt her arms take hold of me. A few seconds later our feet touched the rocks on the side of the bank, and we rose out of the river. Both of us staggered onto the grass and collapsed side by side in a soaking mass of drenched clothes and dripping hair. I turned and looked at the woman next to me who for once waited for me to speak. 'Maggie, thanks for rescuing me. I'm a really poor swimmer; I might have drowned.' She stared back. Her pink and blonde hair was stuck to her face and incredibly she still had her bike helmet on. I started to laugh and so did she. We laughed so hard that we could feel the pain as our bodies convulsed with the sheer joy of it all. It was the most I had laughed since I was a child. Maggie was the only person I had felt happy with since Eve became ill. We eventually pulled ourselves together and attempted to stand up. What a sight we must have been. Like two drowned rats at the side of a river. Maggie finally asked the question I was waiting for.

'Grant, why? Just tell me why you did that.' I shrugged my shoulders and felt like an idiot.

'She was going to drown you, Maggie. I just thought...' My companion put her hand on my shoulder and smiled.

'I know, I know, Grant. Look, let's just get to Lyoncross Wood. No matter what happens now, let's finish our journey. Then you need to go home and get yourself sorted out once and for all.'

'Ok, yes I will. Only one thing, a slight change of plan. Give me this one last wish and I will go to that Lyoncross Wood place you seem so fascinated with; I promise.' Maggie sighed.

'Ok, it's a deal. Tell me what you want but hurry up I am freezing. We need to try and dry ourselves out before we catch our death of cold.'

'We go as far as Bellingham today. It is only another few

hours cycling. We book into a nice hotel and get a decent sleep and a meal. Then tomorrow we can do the last hour to Kielder water via your enchanted forest. How about it?' Maggie looked down at her dripping clothes and then back at me.

'You know what Grant. I am going to accept your offer. Anyway, it's the least I can do after you took me swimming. I think this might be the end of our adventure tomorrow so why not go out in style.'

The rest of the journey took us through a changing landscape of hills and rugged moorland. We would pass large farms that I assumed reared livestock, as well as big houses, tucked away behind small clumps of trees. The rain stayed away, and the wind helped us to dry out. We met few other cyclists and neither of us spoke. It was a case of getting the journey over with as quickly as possible. Of course, we became lost on a few occasions but finally at 4 p.m. in the afternoon we approached the outskirts of Bellingham. All that was left to do was to find a nice hotel and for once on this trip, my luck was in. An ornate sign pointed to a neat little road that wound its way through a large clump of conifer trees. Riverside Hall Hotel beckoned us, and it was a five-star no less.

***

The bath was so full that if I moved the water would slop over the sides. I lay perfectly still and enjoyed the feeling of warmth and peace as the water soothed my aching bones. My thoughts wandered back over the events of the last five days. *Wow, just five days.* Leaving Carrington Drive last Sunday now felt like a lifetime ago. I had looked at Eve's silent and still face and kissed her forehead before I left. *Don't worry my love, I will be back in a week. Try to keep safe and remember that I love you. I always will.* I liked to convince myself that there was a possibility that maybe, just maybe she understood some of the words. The reality was she saw images and heard sounds while she hovered above unable to sort them into any pattern or meaning.

We had been so lucky to get rooms in the Riverside Hall Hotel. Only two were left due to a cancellation so I grabbed them with open arms. It was a big place, maybe it had been some sort of stately home in the past. Large expensive cars lined the driveway outside while elderly couples in elegant summer dresses and open-neck shirts sat sipping coffee in the foyer. I could tell that the gentleman at the reception was not overly keen to accept our custom. To be fair to him, we did look like we had just finished an expedition to the Amazon jungle. 'We don't get many cyclists staying in The Riverside Sir. You might find the Eagle or The Belford in Bellingham to be more suitable for bikes and a lot less expensive.' I suppose I should have given him a look of contempt, but I desperately wanted the rooms. *Keep calm Grant, don't screw this up.* I put on my best false smile before replying.

'Oh no, this will do us fine. A change of clothes and we will fit in perfectly.' I could tell by his smug demeanour that he thought he was about to play his winning hand.

'Well it will be £600 for the two rooms, Sir, is that within your budget?'

'Do you mind taking cash?' I reached into my rucksack and pulled out the damp banknotes before placing them on the counter before him. Thank heaven I had the sense to go to the bank again when we had been in Rothbury. I could have used one of my cards but somehow, I had this ridiculous notion that they might tie me in with Maggie and it could give them clues to her whereabouts. I was starting to enjoy this clandestine creeping around. I felt like a spy, maybe Bond, Grant Bond 005.

Mr. Smug lifted the wad of notes and started to peel them apart so he could count each one. It was hard not to laugh at the look of disgust on his face as little drops of water formed on the counter in front of him. I gave him my best smile before adding, 'Oh, and can you book a table in the restaurant for me and my friend. Let's say 8 o'clock.'

I moved my feet towards the plug and wrapped them around the chain. The water started to drain out of the bath. It was time to smarten up and go down for dinner. Mr. Smug at reception had mentioned it was formal, i.e. no cycling shorts. Luckily, I had a decent pair of jeans with me and a shirt. All I needed to do was iron them dry and I would be ready. Maggie was in the room next door. Before we had parted I had mentioned to her about needing to look ok for dinner.

'I'll be fine Grant. Remember I bought a new dress in

Rothbury. I didn't expect to need it so soon though. See you out here at seven forty-five.'

I sat on the comfortable padded chair in front of the table mirror and counted out what I had left in cash. It was barely £200. Tonight's meal and drinks would have to go on the credit card but at least I would not need to settle up until the morning. We could be away and back into the hills before any alarm was raised. I went to pick up the banknotes and caught my image in the mirror. She was sitting on the end of the bed directly behind me. Her white empty face and pale body were covered by a long elegant red dress. The kind that Eve would have worn if she had been here with me. I did not turn around. Instead, I spoke to the mirror.

'Can you give me one more day, just one more? Let me get to this forest that she wants to go to and then we will part. I could be back by Saturday morning. That's a day earlier. Please, please just allow me this one last day.'

I was sane enough to understand that the insanity was in my head. I knew she would be gone when I turned around to face her. The bed was empty. I also knew she would be back. My guilt would haunt me until I went home. I stood up and walked over to the ornate oak bedroom door. It was time for dinner, oh and drinks. Boy did I need a drink. I knocked at Maggie's room. She answered still dressed in one of the bathrobes the hotel supplied. 'Sorry Grant, I fell asleep. I'll follow you down in twenty minutes. Behave yourself in there.'

The dining room was incredibly elegant. Large windows

looked out onto the perfectly manicured lawn. Ornate drape curtains flowed down the walls to almost touch the richly patterned carpet. Well-dressed couples sat at each of the tables deep in conversation as young women in black dresses carried glasses and plates back and forth to the diners. A few eyes turned to look at me as I was led to a table at the far end of the large room. I studied the wine list and ordered a bottle for £150. This was more like it.

It must have been at least half an hour before she finally arrived. The bottle of wine was nearly finished, and my arm was already waving to one of the waitresses to bring me another. I looked over at the entrance where diners were being met by one of the staff. I was not the only one staring as Maggie was accompanied across the room towards my table. I reckon every other diner was open-mouthed. She had the purple and red-patterned dress on that she had acquired in Rothbury, it was short and showed off her long slim legs. On her feet, she wore a faded pair of white trainers. She had done her hair into a wild spiky fusion. Pink and blonde on top and grey creeping up the sides. Maggie looked perfect. Well, perfect if she had been arriving at Glastonbury for the festival or maybe some hippy commune in the Mojave Desert. I was proud of her though. She looked free and happy. The two of us at that moment were less trapped than everyone else in the room. Two cyclists escaping the world while the waitresses worked, and the old couples tutted their disapproval at us. Maggie beamed a smile at me as she sat down, and I returned the gesture.

Grant

I was a late starter when it came to finding real employment. In the late seventies and into the early eighties much to the growing desperation of my parents, I floated around being a pretend Hells Angel while jumping between poorly paid manual jobs and the dole. Finally, at 23 I decided it was time to grow up and find real work. I enrolled in a government-sponsored electronics course for no other reason than someone on tv said that computers were the future of industry. I have a reasonably structured mind and can work hard when I need to, so I breezed through the course and ended up being employed as an electronics engineer. In those days you could sign on with an agency that would find you a new-full time job every few years. This helped you to move quickly up the salary scale as each company had to offer more than your current salary if they wanted you. I jumped between jobs and even had a brief spell working near London. I finally settled with a nice easy-going firm close to Edinburgh and squeezed out the final years of my twenties enjoying my work. If I am honest, I have to admit that the technical side of things bore me, but the bigwigs seemed to notice that I was good at getting other people to do the actual work and promoted me to be a supervisor.

And so, everything might have remained fine until I decided to jump ship again. The problem was I had got myself into debt by overuse of the then freely available credit cards as well as a mortgage on a flat in Glasgow. I had also met my future wife and needed money to impress her. Off I went to see the agency and they presented me with what they said was an amazing opportunity. My alarm bells were ringing when the agent told me, 'If you can stick a year with this company, I promise you I will be able to get you a job as a people manager with a big firm.' I should have run a mile, but my ego kicked in and I agreed to go for it.

The interview went well. A nice Human Resources lady convinced me I would love working with them and a few days later the contract arrived through my door. I did have a slight feeling of trepidation but nothing, I mean nothing could have prepared me for what I was about to get involved in. The new company was a sub-contract business that manufactured printed circuit boards for bigger and dare I say far more professional establishments. I was immediately put in charge of the test operation with 30 contractors reporting to me. The whole place was run as though the senior managers were in the mafia. Bullying, sacking, racism, sexism, you name it, they did it. At the top of the tree was a man called Lez Bolding or Bolding the Bastard as he was better known. He was utterly ruthless and feared by everyone. Each product we tried to ship would be running late with the constant threat of the company losing the business. The testing bit I had to look after was always under constant pressure. The mafia gang simply saw it as holding up production. They instantly disliked me but then every supervisor was seen as useless by the mafia.

On my first day, my direct line manager ran out of the building screaming. He was later fired as he had taken a nervous breakdown. I spent a few weeks learning the ropes on dayshift while being shouted and swore at by the bosses. The troops who worked for me on the line were lovely. They just tried to survive, and I did my best to look after them. Turnover was horrendous as the bully boys would march along the production lines looking for a reason to flex their muscles and sack somebody. I was finally given the chance to move to nightshift and grabbed the opportunity as it would at least keep me out of the way of the mafia. As soon as I agreed I was told it would be seven nights a week covering twelve-hour shifts from 7 p.m. to 7 a.m. I was promised that this would be only temporary as they only had two nightshift supervisors. The others had either been sacked or quit. Incredibly this was to last for six months. I know it sounds like an exaggeration, but it happened, not a single shift off through the whole winter. This was in 1989, not 1889.

One of the jobs I had to do at the end of my shift was count every single circuit board going through production and leave the report on the senior manager's desks for them coming in on the dayshift. I would start this at 5 a.m. in the hope I could be away just after 7 a.m. before the mafia started to arrive. One morning in the depths of winter after a long 13-

hour shift, I was still trying to complete the count by 8 a.m. I finally finished and raced up the stairs to the manager's office. To my horror, Mr. Lez Bolding was already sitting at his desk. I gingerly placed the report in front of him. He looked up; his big fat face full of malice. 'What the fuck is this?' He picked up the report which ran to about twenty pages and had taken me three hours to do. He then threw it across the room before spitting out his vitriol.

'Get your lazy fucking arse back down there and redo the count. Do it fucking properly this time or don't come back tonight.'

I had to go back down onto the production lines and recount what was a moving target all over again. There was no logic to it, Bolding the Bastard was just showing me he was the boss. I finally crawled home at midday having worked nearly 18 hours and then grabbed five hours of sleep before returning to do it all over again. When I tell this story people say, 'Why did you not just quit?' I had a mortgage and debt. If I had walked out it would have been seen as a failing on my part and getting another job in the industry might have been difficult.

From that point on I decided to fight back. Supervisors would come and go but I managed to survive for a whole year. I was eventually moved back to dayshift and started to put in some structures and systems to make it at least possible to keep count of the various production runs. One day about 8 months after starting I was standing in the canteen smoking a cigarette while studying my clipboard. Bolding the Bastard walked in and immediately went on the attack. A supervisor taking a break was considered a cardinal sin because the place was always in crisis. He stormed up to me, his face red with rage. 'Where are we on E328 boards for IBM?' I looked at my clipboard and then replied.

'372 at test should be complete in 3 hours, 248 at the wave machine should be in test by the end of the shift, and 470 going through cleaning.'

He continued to throw questions at me, and I fenced back with answers to them all. Finally, he stepped away, and his attitude changed to a more conciliatory tone.

'You are going to do well here, Grant.' He then turned and walked away.

From that day on or at least for my final 4 months with the company, I was allowed to become part of the management mafia. I would sit at meetings with them while various poor supervisors and engineers would be torn to bits at production meetings. I hated every minute of it, but I knew my escape plan was coming together. The agent who had promised he would get me a real manager's job if I lasted a year in that hell hole was true to his word.

One morning I phoned in sick. I had an interview with a large corporate company at 9 a.m. that day. It was out in the countryside near the river Clyde and when I drove into the grounds, I was dumbstruck. It was the most beautiful campus I have ever seen. A massive futuristic building covered in miles of dark glass surrounded by tall trees and beautifully manicured lawns. Inside the building was even more incredible. Large plants and small trees surrounded the edge of the productions lines. The offices rose from each side to give a spectacular view of the whole operation. The people who interviewed me were wonderful. I spent the whole day there and had nine separate interviews. I was desperate to start with them and even more desperate to leave Bolding and his hell hole.

A week later the offer arrived at my flat. Bolding and his henchmen tried to talk me into staying with them. No chance. I started with the new company and enjoyed 25 amazing years. It was hard work, but the people were fantastic, every last one of them.

There was to be a twist to this little tale. Around 1995 after I had been there for five years the senior Human resources director asked to see me. 'Grant, a gentleman you might know has applied for a job as a manager here. His name is Lez Bolding and he tells me he worked with you at a previous company. Any thoughts on his suitability?' I won't tell you what my reply was but to this day I feel that I at least got some revenge for all the poor souls who suffered under his regime. I am not a vengeful sort of person though. I do hope he eventually found work again. Maybe counting circuit boards while doing 6 months of 12-hour night shifts.

THUNDERSTRUCK

FRIDAY

It was 8 a.m. in the morning and I felt like shit. At least the girl at reception was not as condescending as her colleague had been the previous day. She spoke in a soft Eastern European accent and could have taught the British a thing or two on how to be customer friendly. Her English was slightly broken but I always feel that adds to the charm. Maggie was already outside wheeling our bikes from the outbuilding the hotel kindly supplied for another £20 per machine. We had agreed that I would settle up the bill while she got the bikes ready. We could then have a relaxing breakfast and be on the road for 9 o'clock.

'That is £815 for dinner and drinks last night, Mr. Ramsey. I hope you and your wife enjoyed evening.' I took a step back. Not because I was suddenly married to Maggie or even the bill I had just been given. It was more to do with the realisation of how much alcohol I must have consumed.

'Can you break that down for me, please? Sorry, what is

your name?' She smiled before replying.

'Sir, yes, of course, Mr. Ramsey. My name Irena. It is £280 for dinner, £450 three bottles of wine, £40 four beer, £30 malt of the month whiskey, and £15 three soft drinks.'

At least I knew now why my head hurt so much. Jesus, three bottles of wine and beers as well. As Irena printed out my bill and ran my card through, I tried to remember last night. I could vaguely recall Maggie staying with me through dinner until I ordered the second bottle and then she retired to her room. I recalled staggering to the guest lounge and drinking more until I probably became a nuisance to the rest of the clientele. In my defence, I knew I would sleep right through if I was drunk. At least that way the porcelain lady would not be able to infiltrate my brain. I don't remember getting to my room, but it seems like my guardian angel appeared just as the bar staff were about to throw me out of the hotel. Maggie guided me to my bed and even helped me take off my shoes before leaving me to sleep it off. The dinner was nice though, or so Maggie told me. Oh, and to prove I do have some self-control the third bottle of wine was on the bedside cabinet this morning only half empty. I must have decided to stop drinking and get some sleep. Either that or I passed out, I shall leave you to decide.

'Would you like receipt Mr. Ramsey, Sir?'

I wasn't listening to Irena anymore. Two men were standing to my left talking to a second female receptionist. The foyer was busy, so it was difficult to hear what they were saying. He was holding out a leather wallet towards the young lady. I had seen this action so many times in films and television to know they were plainclothes policemen.

'Erm, no thank you, Irena.' I tried to smile and act nonchalant before walking slowly towards the main entrance doors. One of the men glanced at me as I left. He nudged his colleague, but I was already outside before I could see if they followed. Maggie was walking towards me having decanted the bikes against a wall beside the lawn. I looked back and sighed with relief when no one appeared through the exit.

'What's up Grant. You look like you've seen a ghost. Or was it the wine you drank last night?' She chuckled at her little comment.

'Forget breakfast. We need to go, Maggie. The police have just turned up.' I could tell by the look on her face that she thought I was over-reacting.

'Are you sure, Grant? I mean do you really think they are looking for me. It could be nothing to do with me and Vincent.' I knew I was right though and took her arm before marching over to our bikes.

'Maggie, we need to go. Do you want to be arrested here? This is our last chance to make it to that forest you want to see, and I want to get to Kielder Dam. Look, I just need one more day. I don't even care where we go.' She nodded and took my hand.

'It's ok, Grant. Yes, one more day. Lyoncross Wood and then onto the dam. Maybe we could even sleep outside again tonight, and I will hand myself over to the authorities tomorrow. I squeezed her hand and nodded. But I knew that our journey would end today. I had already promised the porcelain lady and she would not accept any more excuses. Not without serious retribution anyway.

The sky was heavy as we crept through Bellingham. It seemed to be no more than a large village and even at 8 a.m. in the morning it was already busy with walkers and a few cyclists. The town is a popular stop-off point on the Pennine way although I doubt that many of them would have been staying in the Riverside Hall Hotel last night or scoffing £150 bottles of wine. It was still very warm, a brooding sort of day. One that felt like it could blow up into a lightning storm before soaking the poor unfortunate souls below with warm rain. A little row of old-fashioned shops lined the main street. We found a café and waited in the inevitable queue for coffee. I stood nervously trying to keep below the radar and not talk to anyone. Maggie of course was chatting away with whoever would listen to her. She seemed so happy and carefree despite the trouble she was in. Having picked up our drinks we slipped down a side street away from the throng and sat down against a low stone wall.

'Maggie, I am sorry I got so drunk last night.' She nudged me with her arm.

'Don't worry about it, Grant. After so many years of caring for Eve, you deserve to let your hair down. I know you miss her as well. In a few days, you'll be home and back together again.'

'Yes, I suppose you are right. I just wish I had not fallen out with Robbie. In fact, I wish I had not fallen out with everyone. I suppose I just lashed out at those I loved.' Maggie placed her head on my shoulder.

'Look, you might not realise it right now, Grant, but you are a nice guy. You are doing your best for Eve.' *Why did I not feel so sure about that? I wanted to go home but then I didn't.* I turned towards my companion.

'Maggie, are you not afraid of what will happen to you when the police catch up? I mean you told me you wrapped his body in sheets. They will want to know why and also why you didn't report what happened. I am worried for you; you are going to have a lot of explaining to do.' She shrugged her shoulders and seemed unconcerned.

'Who cares? It won't be any worse than having to live with him. I covered Vincent with the sheets because I didn't want to have to look at him while I packed to leave. I kept thinking that he might suddenly tell me I was useless and could not go away on my own.' She pondered as if lost in thought for a few seconds. 'I wish I had met someone normal like you Grant. Maybe life would have been so different.'

'I am going to help you, Maggie, no matter what happens. I have money, loads of it and nothing to spend it on. I will pay for a lawyer, whatever it takes to get you out of this mess.' She looked into my eyes before replying.

'You don't need to do that. Just go home and sort your

life out. I can look after myself.'

'Maggie, I will help you because you have helped me. Getting my life sorted out has already started. It did the day I met you.'

We said no more and sat for the next few minutes finishing our drinks. It was only ten miles to Kielder Dam; we would be there by midday. On the opposite side of the road stood a line of terraced stone houses. A figure was standing in the shadows just behind the large window in the one in front of us. It was difficult to make them out, but I knew who it was. I had come to know that silhouette. The clock was running down. We were both being hunted, Maggie by the law and me by my guilt. It was time to make our last break for freedom. I stood up and she followed. Within minutes we were back out in the open countryside crossing a stone bridge over the River North Tyne.

Our route would follow the river all the way to Kielder Dam gradually gaining height with each passing mile. Farming land bordered the edges of the North Tyne, but steep forested hills rose oppressively on each side once the cultivated land petered out. There were few villages of any size after Bellingham. Just some scattered settlements and farms to break up the monotony of fields and hills. I was desperate to do a pee. It was my own fault for drinking a massive coffee. Despite the remoteness, each time I spied a spot I could use another walker or cyclist would appear. I was becoming desperate when at last the road caught the edge of a forest.

'Maggie, I need to pee, wait here for me.' She pulled her bike up and sat down on the grass verge.

'I need to do one as well. I'm not used to drinking coffee, it's your fault.'

'Ok, wait here and then I'll watch out for you when I come back.'

'Be careful in there Grant, you know what you're like.'

I ignored the comment and climbed over the wire fence. Unfortunately, my leg became caught and I tumbled into the grass on the other side. Despite immediately jumping up I could hear Maggie chuckling. I felt self-conscious doing a pee within earshot of her, so I squeezed through the tightly packed trees and went deeper into the forest. The relief was palpable as I relieved myself against one of the trees. My eyes caught something moving through the wood about 20 yards away. It was her. She was following our every step, keeping parallel until the time came to strike. Gliding along in our shadow. I finished as quickly as possible and made my way back to the road.

'Ok, my turn now.' I jumped the fence on one stride, this time without falling.

'Not here, Maggie. We need to go. Trust me.' She shrugged and started to pedal away. I think my companion was becoming used to me acting strangely neurotic.

'Alright, Grant. But if I wet myself it's your fault.'

We cycled on for a mile or so further but the opportunity for Maggie didn't arrive and then astonishingly at a tiny village called Hesleydale we spotted a sign pointing to public toilets. A neat little picnic area with two wooden tables sat surrounded by a few houses. A couple with young children occupied one of the tables. We parked our bikes and I sat down at a bench to wait for Maggie. It still felt warm and clammy, but the air was heavy. That storm was coming, I just knew it. Maybe it would be a fitting end to our journey. It could only be a few more miles to Lyoncross Wood and the Dam.

The family at the other table headed off and drove away in one of the two vehicles in the little car park. Suddenly a scream pierced the air, it was Maggie and coming from the toilet building. I jumped to my feet and raced over to the door marked Female. I crashed into the wooden frame so hard that it gave way and my body tumbled onto the floor. The momentum carried me sliding across the tiles until I eventually hit the wall on the opposite side. It took a few seconds for my eyes to focus as I looked up from where I had landed. Two women stood staring at me, one with shock and the other with a resigned concern. Maggie spoke first.

'Grant, can you believe it. This lady here is Phylis Nims, we used to go to rock concerts together when we were young. We saw Depeche Mode and even The Buzzcocks in Carlisle, how yowzer bloody amazing is that. What are the chances we would meet in a remote place like this.' Phylis Nims still looked shocked at my spectacular entrance but she managed to mumble a few words while she tried to recover.

'Hi, it's nice to meet you, Grant.' I stood up and offered to shake her hand. The poor woman was chalk white. It was hard not to laugh. Maggie was twittering away as though a man crashing through the door of a woman's toilet in the middle of nowhere was a perfectly normal occurrence. Making a fool of myself was becoming a habit, but I didn't care. *Just get to the end of the journey today Grant and as soon as you are on your way back to Eve, the ghost will disappear.* I dusted myself down and waited outside for Maggie. It was another twenty minutes before she appeared. I could hear her and Phylis Nims laughing as they recalled happier times. It made me feel good listening to their voices even if I could not make out the words.

***

We left Hesleydale just as the first drops of rain started to fall. The sky was black and angry, a fitting backdrop to mirror how I was feeling. I could see the police car pulling into the car park at the public toilets just as we disappeared down the track. The net was closing in on both of us. I knew the Porcelain lady was near, I could sense her watching our every move. It was barely five miles to the dam although only half of that would be needed to get to Lyoncross Wood. I no longer cared about going any further. Once we had made Maggie's goal, I knew we had to go back to Bellingham, the nearest large settlement, and hand her over to the police.

Our path followed the winding country lanes, sandwiched

on either side by large mostly barren hills. Maggie had not spoken a word since leaving Bellingham. As we trundled up yet another gradient the track made a sharp turn to reveal a small forest a few hundred yards away on our right-hand side. I pulled my bike up just as the first crack of thunder roared through the air. 'Maggie, Maggie, I think this is it. The place you wanted to get to.' We bundled our bikes off the road and left them propped against a low brick wall. The rain was now coming down hard, bouncing off the tarmac like a million translucent bullets. It was difficult to be heard over the noise of both that and the now increasing thunderclaps.

'We need to find shelter before we are either drowned or electrocuted.' A clump of yellow and purple bushes shadowed by two small trees looked to be our best bet. It was too dangerous to make the dash for the larger shelter of Lyoncross Wood until the storm had passed. We tumbled into the bushes and huddled together to ride out the deluge. Her face was only inches from mine. Water dripped from the end of her nose and down her cheeks.

'Well, this is it, Maggie. I think this is the end of our journey.' She looked up at the dark sky and sighed.

'Grant, I was thinking, well I was wondering, what if.' Her words petered out as if she was scared to go on.

'Yes, what is it? It's ok Maggie, tell me.'

'It's just that this journey and meeting you has been like a different life for me. I enjoy your company; you are a good man. Maybe I could come back to Glasgow with you. I could help you look after Eve. Be a sort of housekeeper. Unpaid of course, I just don't want to be on my own again.' I was taken aback by her request. Maybe I should have considered my answer a bit more before replying, but what she was asking was crazy.

'Maggie, think about it. I am a married man. What would my brother Robbie think and the rest of the family for that matter? Look, we can still keep in contact. I have money, I will get you sorted out with the Vincent thing. But, no, what you ask is not possible.' I could see tears running down her face now, mingling with the rain.

'I know Grant, I know. It was just a thought, a crazy thought, I'm sorry.'

I pulled her close to me and we remained huddled together in silence as the thunder cracks became more frequent. Shards of white lightning flashed across the gloom that now covered the landscape. In the distance, I could make out her outline silhouetted against the trees of Lyoncross Wood. She was waiting for us to make our final move.

The headlights of two cars could be seen edging along the narrow road. As they neared our two bikes standing against the wall they pulled up. A man got out of the first one and dragged his coat over his head. He walked towards the bikes and studied them before scanning the forest in the distance. In the gloom, he could not see the two of us huddled in the bushes just a few yards away. He ran back to the car and pointed to the trees. Three more bodies climbed out of the cars, two of them in uniform including a woman. I turned to Maggie who was watching with a look of horror on her face.

'This is it, Maggie. There's no point in running anymore. Let's get this over with, the sooner the better.' She started to stand up.

'No Grant. I came this far; I am finishing at Lyoncross Wood no matter what it takes.' Suddenly she was on her feet fleeing through the gorse bushes and grass towards the little forest. I could see the police looking on in amazement. I too was running, chasing after Maggie as she dashed towards the trees and the glowing silhouette of the Porcelain lady reflected in the lightning. I finally caught her as she reached the edge of the wood and we collapsed in a soaking heap on the ground. A lightning bolt streaked against the trees sending a large branch crashing onto the forest floor. The rain lashed down upon both of us. We finally got back to our feet just as the posse of police arrived. One of them moved forward towards me. He was red-faced and breathing heavily as he spoke.

'Grant Ramsey, I assume you are the elusive Grant Ramsey we have been searching for?' I stared at him in confusion. It was Maggie they wanted, not me.

'Yes, yes, I am Grant Ramsey, what's wrong? Have I done something?' The rain was running down his face as the six soaking figures stood facing each other in the storm.

'Mr. Ramsey, you are under arrest for the murder of Eve Ramsey. You do not have to say anything. But, it may harm your defence if you do not mention when questioned something which you later rely on in court. Anything you do say may be given in evidence.' Do you understand?'

They turned me around and placed a pair of handcuffs onto my wrists. I took one look at Maggie as they led me away. She watched white-faced in disbelief while the porcelain lady faded into the background to finally disappear inside the mist and the rain.

WHISPER

I am not here to beg for your sympathy. What I do ask is that you listen to the end of my tale and try to understand how this all came about. You can make your own judgement on whether I am a good or a bad person although I doubt that either conclusion will fit comfortably with you. I could sense that it didn't with the jury I faced either, but they could only really give one verdict. I knew that. We just had to go through the charade to make sure that the legal system was played out in full. Oh, and yes, the judge and the lawyers, as well as everyone else involved in the process needed to earn their money. I hadn't been in a court since I had done jury duty in my twenties. I was amazed to see that they still wore those old itchy looking wigs. I suppose that is why they get paid so much. They probably get double time and a wig bonus on top.

Prison life is not what they show you on tv. I was expecting everyone to be wearing blue overalls and lounging about watching big flat-screen televisions while they searched for a file hidden inside a cake the wife had just delivered. Well, it's not like that one bit. You get to wear your own clothes, and you might even be allowed to watch Coronation Street on a tiny tv set if you behave yourself. When I first arrived here, I had to share a cell with another inmate. It was fine but the shared toilet thing in the cell is the problem. It is covered by a curtain, but the smell can be rather unpleasant. They eventually moved me to a cell in what they call a ward so I could be on my own. It's ok but it means I get less interaction with the other guys and I have to go through some weird counselling sessions. I am not sure why; I assume they think I have some sort of psychological issues. Maybe I have, who knows?

Yes, I did it, but how can anyone say I acted on my own? Eve might not have been able to talk or even hear but her eyes still held life and our minds will always be joined together. I suppose my longer sentence is down to the fact that they claimed it was a premeditated act. Of course, it was. I planned the date, even the time that I would switch off Eve's existence. We had talked about it in the days when she was still lucid. We both agreed it had to happen. We never spoke about the actual act or how I would do it, but the plan had always been for me to follow her. Right up until the police arrested me, I had intended to fulfil my part of the agreement. At the end of my week of freedom roaming the Borders on my bike, I had expected to go back to Carrington Drive and finish my part of the pact.

How was I to know that Robbie would send Mandy around to check on Eve? When there was no answer, they called her sister Kate. All hell broke loose when she said she had never been asked to look after Eve while I was away. He always was an interfering know all my brother Robbie. I still love him though and I think he feels the same. Actually, it's probably more sympathy than love with him, but I'll take that. He has even been in to visit me a few times. The nice people in the prison supply a Perspex screen to keep us separated while we chat. It's great as it means I can't belt him on the nose while he lectures me about getting my life together.

I had expected to hear from Maggie at first, maybe even get a visit from her. There was no sign though until I had been in prison for six months when a letter arrived. It seems that she did eventually hand herself in after staying out on the road for a few more weeks. She too ended up going through a court case. The final result saw her being found guilty of not reporting a death but other than a stern talking to the judge had been sympathetic with her case. Her stepson Moonie sadly died of a drug overdose around the same time. Maggie told me she had found a part-time job and was also working as a volunteer helping women recover from abusive relationships. I knew she would be good at that sort of thing. Maggie had such a kind heart; I do miss her. I wrote back but that was a few years ago so I suppose she must have moved on. Maybe she was one of those who could not forgive me for what I did. I like to think it was more to do with the fact that I never told her what had happened while we were together for those few days. How could I though? At the time even I did not know what I had done.

I think I mentioned to you that they tend to keep me

isolated from the rest of the inmates because I have issues. Well according to them, personally I feel completely normal. Do you believe in the afterlife? You know that thing where you are born again and get to live your life all over but as someone else. I do. You see the Porcelain lady sits on her chair in the corner of my cell. She is with me all the time, that is why I never feel lonely. When she first arrived, she still looked the same. A face with all the contours but no openings for her mouth, her eyes, her nose, or her ears. It was like that for months and then one morning after I had been out for exercise in the yard I came back in and discovered something amazing. Where her mouth should have been, I noticed the tiniest of cracks. It would increase ever so slightly each day. Then after a month or two, the aperture was wide enough for it to move. One night before lights out I put my ear to her mouth and listened. The faintest weakest whisper floated between the two of us.

'It's me, It's Eve. I will always love you.'

ALL OF MY PREVIOUS FIVE BOOKS ARE
AVAILABLE FROM AMAZON OR AT
RMPEARSON.NET

THE PATH

THE MOUNTAINS WILL NOT HIDE HIS SECRET. TWO MEN ON THE RUN, BUT WHAT IS IT THAT FOLLOWS THEM?

Neurotic Ralph and easy-going Harvey are trying to escape from their past in the desolate mountains of Scotland. Not only are they alcoholics but one of them holds a terrible secret he is desperate to leave behind. But something is following them, and it is seeking revenge. Their journey will turn into a living nightmare and survival for one of them may mean the end for the other.

You cannot run forever. At some point, the only way to have a future is to turn and face the past.

DEADWATER

TWO BROTHERS, ONE INHERITANCE. A CLASSIC DARK TALE OF DECEIT AND REVENGE FROM THE GRAVE

Who would dare unlock the secret of Deadwater House?
The rumour had cast a shadow over the village for as long as anyone could remember. Who was the ghostly child that watched from the window of the Denham-Granger mansion? The truth would turn out to be far worse than any of the locals could ever have imagined. Whatever had been caged for so long wanted revenge and now it was hunting its prey down. Only one person stood in the way, reluctant local policeman, Gordon Chisholme. Soon he would have to face the truth. It had already turned its attention to him, and he could feel its icy grip reaching out for the next victim.

BROKEN LEAVES

ONLY SHE KNOWS THE TERRIBLE SECRET OF HIS PAST.

Blackmail, Murder, Love, Hate.

There is nowhere left to hide when revenge comes calling.

One moment of madness in his youth has caught up with Matt Cunningham. The only person who can save the successful business executive is his ex-lover, Roni Paterson. But how do you find the woman who has disappeared for thirty years and what if she becomes part of the unfolding nightmare?

A dark thriller to keep you reading through the night.

A SEASON FOR GHOSTS

FOUR SEASONS, NINE DARK TALES

Step into the shadow.

Who is the mysterious woman watching from a distance each time Robert goes out on a date? Why do the snow people haunt the isolated railway station? Will Lord Blackbarron make it through 800 miles of frozen wasteland before the Ice Ghosts catch him? What is it that the baby whispers? And if you survive, then pray you never have to meet, the Tall Man.

Nine stories to keep you awake at night. Nine dark tales to haunt your dreams.

SEVEN HUNDRED YEARS OF WAITING. ONE-QUARTER OF A MILLION DAYS TO DREAM OF DEATH AND DESTRUCTION.

For seven long centuries, Luka rotted in the cave. Damned to wait in that hidden hell hole while Raso, the man who had betrayed him walked free. In the distant village, his wife grew old and passed away while his son fathered children of his own. Each generation lived and died until they too became ghosts of the past. But the unknown soldier did not forget. He counted every single bleak day, waiting for the moment when he would have his revenge.

As 1965 dawned Luka surveyed the distant village from his prison. Today would be different. After nearly seven hundred years the wait was over. The man Luka hated was back and even though others would have to die, bitter revenge would finally be his.

William Wallace was supposed to have said, 'You can take our lives, but you can never take our freedom.' He was lying, he needed both.

Selected Amazon Reviews

This is a book that managed to affect me deeply. Acutely thoughtful and at times really creepy, *The Path* is a ghost story that is at once desperately sad but also ultimately uplifting, and, in its own way, also cosy and comforting. I read loads of ghost stories every year- this is one of my favourites. (The Path)

**

Loved this book. I've read a few books from this author and I thought it would be hard to beat *Deadwater,* but this book has been by far the best. It was comical, enlightening, thoughtful, and scary. You get really involved with the characters. Would highly recommend (Scotland Shall Burn)

**

What an anthology. One of the best of the year for me. A style of book I haven't seen before as the author includes a written musing on the seasons of the year, between every two to three tales. This works so well it's almost worth the price of the book for these alone. There are no weak stories here, but three, in particular, stand out, what a clever baby will make you look at all infants in a brand-new light, Our lady of the Quarry is a belter of a ghost story with a stunning twist. Harmonica seeks partner tells the heart-breaking tale of a lonely man and a homeless woman and how we all judge without knowing the whole story. All in all, 5 stars are not enough for this collection of tales. Would like to see more from this author. Here's hoping. (A Season for Ghosts)

***

The author details a thrilling story of the downfall of a successful Scottish businessman who chases his past to stop the destruction of his seemingly perfect life. Brilliantly written, with characters I really connected to. I couldn't put it down! (Broken Leaves)

***

One of the best books I've read for a long time. The characters were interesting, and I really felt a personal affiliation with the main ones. Rooting them to do well or in a few cases...rooting for their demise.

It's great when you get so involved in a story that you stay up late reading it. There were some surprises, sad and happy moments. The era was well captured, bringing back memories of local police stations, village life and there was always a haunted house growing up. Loved this. Can't wait to read the next one (Deadwater)

Printed in Great Britain
by Amazon